Kith & Kin

The Kerrigan Kids, Volume 3

W.J. May

Published by Dark Shadow Publishing, 2020.

KITH & KIN

First edition. January 15, 2020.

Written by W.J. May.

Also by W.J. May

Bit-Lit Series
Lost Vampire
Cost of Blood
Price of Death

Blood Red Series
Courage Runs Red
The Night Watch
Marked by Courage
Forever Night
The Other Side of Fear
Blood Red Box Set Books #1-5

Daughters of Darkness: Victoria's Journey
Victoria
Huntress
Coveted (A Vampire & Paranormal Romance)
Twisted
Daughter of Darkness - Victoria - Box Set

Castle of Power
Limits of Magic
Protectors of Light

Omega Queen Series
Discipline
Bravery
Courage

Paranormal Huntress Series
Never Look Back
Coven Master
Alpha's Permission
Blood Bonding
Oracle of Nightmares
Shadows in the Night
Paranormal Huntress BOX SET #1-3

Prophecy Series
Only the Beginning
White Winter
Secrets of Destiny

Royal Factions
The Price For Peace
The Cost for Surviving

The Chronicles of Kerrigan
Rae of Hope
Dark Nebula
House of Cards
~~Royal Tea~~
Under Fire
End in Sight
Hidden Darkness
Twisted Together
Mark of Fate
Strength & Power
Last One Standing
Rae of Light
The Chronicles of Kerrigan Box Set Books # 1 - 6

The Chronicles of Kerrigan: Gabriel
Living in the Past
Present For Today
Staring at the Future

The Chronicles of Kerrigan Prequel
Christmas Before the Magic
Question the Darkness
Into the Darkness
Fight the Darkness
Alone in the Darkness
Lost in Darkness
The Chronicles of Kerrigan Prequel Series Books #1-3

The Chronicles of Kerrigan Sequel
A Matter of Time
Time Piece
Second Chance
Glitch in Time
Our Time
Precious Time

The Hidden Secrets Saga
Seventh Mark (part 1 & 2)

The Kerrigan Kids
School of Potential
Myths & Magic
Kith & Kin
Playing With Power

The Queen's Alpha Series
Eternal
Everlasting
Unceasing
Evermore
Forever
Boundless
Prophecy
Protected

Foretelling
Revelation
Betrayal
Resolved

The Senseless Series
Radium Halos - Part 1
Radium Halos - Part 2
Nonsense
Perception
The Senseless - Box Set Books #1-4

Standalone
Shadow of Doubt (Part 1 & 2)
Five Shades of Fantasy
Shadow of Doubt - Part 1
Shadow of Doubt - Part 2
Four and a Half Shades of Fantasy
Dream Fighter
What Creeps in the Night
Forest of the Forbidden
Arcane Forest: A Fantasy Anthology
The First Fantasy Box Set

Watch for more at www.wjmaybooks.com.

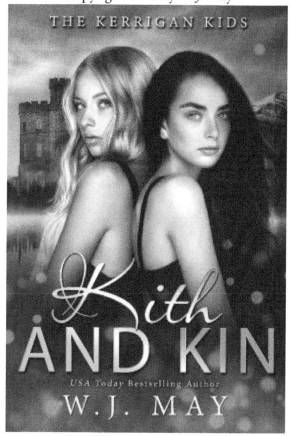

Have You Read the C.o.K Series?

The Prequel series is a Sub-Series of the Chronicles of Kerrigan.
The prequel on how Simon Kerrigan met Beth!!
Download for FREE:

THE CHRONICLES OF KERRIGAN: PREQUEL –
Christmas Before the Magic
Question the Darkness
Into the Darkness
Fight the Darkness
Alone in the Darkness
Lost the Darkness

THE CHRONICLES OF KERRIGAN

THE CHRONICLES OF KERRIGAN SEQUEL

Matter of Time
Time Piece
Second Chance
Glitch in Time
Our Time
Precious Time

The Chronicles of Kerrigan: Gabriel

Living in the Past

Present for Today

Staring at the Future

Kerrigan Chronicles

Book 1 – Stopping Time
Book 2 – A Passage of Time
Book 3 – Ticking Clock
Book 4 – Just in Time
Book 5 – Time in the City
Book 6 – Ultimate Future

The Kerrigan Kids Series

Find W.J. May

Website:
https://www.wjmaybooks.com
Facebook:
https://www.facebook.com/pages/Author-WJ-May-FAN-PAGE/
141170442608149
Newsletter:
SIGN UP FOR W.J. May's Newsletter to find out about new releases, updates, cover reveals and even freebies!
http://eepurl.com/97aYf

Kith & Kin

IF YOU CAN'T BEAT THEM, join them...

When yet another attack leaves the students of Guilder Boarding School looking for answers, Aria decides to take matters into her own hands. Armed with a set of powers she'd vowed never to use, she follows the clues to the killer—only to find that nothing is as it seems.

The world is changing. Alliances are shifting. And the very foundations of the supernatural community are at risk. Like it or not, people are starting to take sides.

But will Aria and her friends find themselves on the right side of the fight?

Or are some sins too big to come back from?

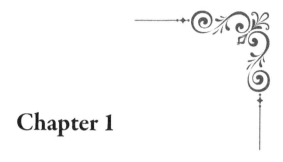

Chapter 1

To anyone watching from the air, something incredible was happening on the secretive campus of Guilder Boarding School. Bolts of lightning ripped through the peaceful night, feral growls and roars echoed off the trees. But perhaps the most fantastical sight of all was happening a little ways off from the rest of the action. A soft golden glow, tucked away in the shadowy trees.

"Come on," Aria whispered, bowing her head. "*Please* work."

Her eyes were closed and her body was frozen in suspension, as if the ethereal light radiating from her fingers had put the world in a kind of trance. Both hands were pressing on the chest of the boy lying beneath her. The same boy whose broken kiss still lingered on her lips.

He'd passed out only a moment after, staying conscious just long enough to stare up at her with a silent goodbye. Then the pain and blood loss overtook him, leaving her alone to perform a magical miracle on the dark and wintery night.

"Just stay with me," she whispered again, leaning over as locks of her dark hair whispered around his face. "Just keep breathing."

Never had she been able to work the tatù until that very moment. Never had she understood that such a magic had a cost. It wasn't possible to simply save someone's life with a wave of one's hands. Such a thing demanded personal sacrifice. A life to be leveraged against the one to be lost.

It consumed her completely, leaving her immune to the world around her. To the vicious fight raging on in the trees. A fight that was about to get a whole lot bigger.

"Benji!"

Lily was the first to arrive in the clearing—ironic, given that she was one of the only people involved who wasn't in possession of a speed tatù. She raced across the lawns, her shimmering gown trailing behind her, then froze in horror at the nightmarish scene.

Two of her friends were lying on the ground, soaked in blood she could only pray wasn't their own. Haloed in a fantastical ring of light that was—for the moment—keeping them alive.

...her other friend was fighting a tiger.

"Ben!" she screamed again, prioritizing in terms of risk.

Without a thought she went tearing towards him, ignoring his warning, looking around for something she could use to fight. Then all at once, an enormous shadow stepped in between them.

At first, she didn't understand what she was staring at. There was something obvious and familiar about it, but her mind couldn't force it through. She tilted her head, trying to see to the very top. Then the creature let out a deafening roar—just inches from her face.

"...that's a bear."

She didn't know who she was talking to. The others were either locked in a death-match or lost in some supernatural trance. But, as she'd later realize, it was impossible to come face-to-face with such a creature without stating the obvious at least once.

She allowed herself one scream. Then she grabbed a jagged tree branch off the ground.

"Fire!" she called, lifting it high above her head.

Benji tore his eyes away from the tiger, glancing over his shoulder, before firing off a bolt of lightning with his free hand. He was already back in the fight by the time it hit the target. He didn't see the edge of the branch burst into flames, or the girl in the ball gown swing it fiercely at the bear.

He hadn't even had the time to check on the others, though they were no longer talking, and in his periphery they'd grown terrifyingly still. His every attention was fixed on the wild beast in front of him. The one that kept getting back to its feet, no matter how many times lightning struck.

"Just stay down!" he shouted in frustration, pushing back a tangle of damp hair and wishing like crazy he wasn't still wearing a suit. "For shit's sake, Alexander!"

Of course, he had no way of knowing whether it was Alexander. He'd heard some shouting and arrived at a fight already in progress. But he didn't see who else it could be. And he didn't know anyone else who wouldn't hesitate in doling out such lethal force.

...therein lies the problem.

As the tiger sprang at him once again, he caught it mid-air with another searing volt of electricity. It wrapped around the beast's body, twisting and writhing before it collapsed upon the ground with a high-pitched snarl. A painful shot, like all the others that had come before, but just seconds later it was scrambling back up to its feet—ready to try again.

Yes, lethal force was the problem. Benji couldn't bring himself to use it. And as long as he pulled his punches, the beast would keep getting up. And as long as it kept getting up, it would keep jumping at him. And eventually, he would tire. His arms were already beginning to shake.

"What the hell is wrong with you!" he shouted, leaping back with a curse as the beast darted close enough to swipe at his legs. "You're actually trying to *kill* us right here on the lawn?!"

The tiger couldn't answer, but its eyes glowed with frenzied rage. The kind of rage it might have had the sense to stop otherwise, but had grown in panic beyond his control. Again and again he sprang at the boy with the lightning, growing more manic and feral with each pass.

Eventually, he had to stop. Eventually, he would tire.

"You guys?" another voice rang suddenly through the trees. This one was younger, trying to be brave but full of fear. "What's going—"

James trailed off when he raced into the clearing, his slick formal shoes scrambling to a hasty stop. At first, he simply didn't understand what he was seeing. Benji was fighting a tiger. Lily was fending off a bear. His sister and Jason were locked in some kind of celestial mind-meld.

And the worst part? None of them had seen what else was coming through the trees.

It's mine, then. He ripped off his coat, swallowing hard. *I'll take care of it...*

ARIA STAYED EXACTLY where she was, never blinking, never moving. Despite the throbbing pain in her head and the intense cold creeping up her legs, she was only barely aware of the world around her. There was a violent scuffle. Something that sounded almost like a bear?

She never saw it. She had eyes for only one man.

The tatù might have been working slowly, but it *was* working. Jason's suit was still in tatters, but the skin beneath it had begun to repair. She watched as his chest stitched itself together, and the giant gashes trailing from his chin to his navel began to slowly fade away.

It was utterly surreal.

She could feel his body as well as her own. Each breath. Each beat of his heart. It was as if by healing the damage in him, she was repairing herself as well. As if their connection went beyond kith and kin, to something deeper. Something that had always been waiting, deep inside.

He pulled in a sharp gasp, eyes fluttering open in a daze.

"...Arie?"

There was a pause in the rhythm of her hands. For a moment, the light around them flickered. It was so quiet, she couldn't be sure she'd actually heard it. So weak, it was hardly there.

"I'm here," she breathed, clasping his hand. "I'm right—"

Only then did she realize how utterly exhausted she was. A wave of deadening fatigue took hold and she fell in a pile beside him—pressing her cheek into the thin layer of ice covering the grass. The world tilted, but didn't disappear. All at once, she realized something else was happening.

There was a bear. And Lily was fighting it...with a stick?

She tilted her head to the side, wondering if she was dreaming. The lovely girl was leaping back and forth in her ball gown, waving a torch between them, dancing just out of reach. It was only a matter of time before the unthinkable happened. But at least for now she was safe.

If only the same could be said for the others.

Her little brother was backing slowly into the clearing, his hands lifted in the air, his lips fluttering with quiet supplications. Though Aria couldn't hear what they were. She twisted her head, trying desperately to see what he was looking at. Then her body froze with sudden dread.

There wasn't just one tiger. There were two.

And both were heading straight for Benji.

No!

James did his best—considering he was a young teenager with no weapons or powers. At the last minute he let out a yell and charged the beast with his bare hands, but the tiger leapt lightly over his head, aiming for the man throwing lightning bolts on the other side.

The fight between Benji and Alexander was getting bloodier the longer it went on. Sometime in the last few minutes the tiger had managed to get in a strike or two, but it was clear that Benji was dominating. Never had Aria seen such a look on his face. The man was incensed—eyes locked on the tiger, though his mind was still swimming with images of his mangled best friend.

He didn't see the other tiger leaping towards him. He didn't hear James' cry of warning until it was already too late. His hand was lifted high, about to call down another blast of lightning, when the tiger streaked out of the darkness, closing its jaws around his unprotected arm.

He let out a shout, more surprise than pain, then whipped around to see what had grabbed him. In the same instant the tiger yanked him right off his feet, dragging him out of the trees.

"No!" Aria screamed. "Benji!"

Alexander was standing in the middle of the clearing, panting softly, trying to catch his breath. The tips of his ivory fur were singed and smoking. His snowy paws were tinged with blood. He met Aria's gaze for only a split second before drifting to the boy lying by her side.

Jason's eyes were open, but he wasn't registering anything around him. While the night would be forever burned into the others' memories, most everything past that initial moment would be lost to him in shock. His hand drifted to the scratches raked down his body. His head lifted weakly, then fell back onto the grass. When he let out a quiet moan, the tiger took a sudden step.

For a split second, Aria was terrified he was going to attack again. Jason was in no position to defend himself, and she doubted she could even lift her arms. Her eyes widened as he stalked towards them in the snow, unseen by the others.

Benji was gone. James had taken off after him. Lily was still doing her best to ward off the bear. There was no one left to see what was happening. No one powerful enough to make it stop.

He took a step closer. Then another step after that. Silent as a ghost. An unfathomable expression in his eyes. Without looking away for an instant Aria reached out and took Jason's hand, wrapping her fingers tightly through his. She doubted he'd even notice. But it was all the tiger could see. He stared for another moment, then lifted his head suddenly and took off into the trees.

Aria stared after him in shock, too overwhelmed to move.

The seconds crawled by like hours. Every minute felt like years. Then, all at once, a series of distant shouts rang through the trees as a dozen footsteps pounded towards them. There was a tiny gasp as the bear vanished. Lily dropped the torch, which promptly extinguished in the snow.

Just a few seconds later, the glow from an array of flashlights began darting through the trees. Aria winced weakly, squinting into the light of the glaring beams, before they lowered in unison and she saw half of the junior class standing in front of her.

Tiffany, Oliver, and Milo were standing near the front—looking a little tipsy, like someone had spiked the punch. Catalina and Lisette were just behind, elbowing their way forward.

They'd surged forward at the same time but then stopped at the same time as well, staring out over the clearing in absolute horror. A dozen pairs of eyes shot in a dozen directions, but none of them seemed to know where to land. Was it the mangled teenagers, or the fact that the ground was covered in ice? Or was it the fact that the ice was drenched in blood?

No one said a word. No one tried to answer the silent question. Instead they simply stood in a shivering mass of tuxedos and ball gowns, trying to keep grounded, frozen in fright.

More people were running up behind them. Typical faculty robes. Aria could see Luke's face among them. No doubt her parents had been called and weren't far behind.

"Aria?"

Catalina took a shaky step forward, clutching something in her hand. It took Aria's eyes a moment to focus on the blur of spikes and sparkles before she realized it was a crown.

"What are you doing here?"

A rather odd question. One that probably would have made a lot more sense the other way around. But no one seemed to notice. They couldn't stop staring at the blood.

"We came to find you," Catalina whispered. "You were named Winter Queen."

Chapter 2

That was the last thing Aria remembered. The sight of that sparkling tiara dropping to the ground. Everything else was just flashes—so hazy and blurred there was a decent chance her shell-shocked mind had simply made the whole thing up.

Her head had dropped weakly to the grass, and by the time she lifted it again the area was swarming with people. The alarm had been sounded and every person currently on the campus of Guilder came pouring out onto the lawn. Agents were sealing a perimeter. Students were being herded back to the dance. Lily was sitting just a few feet away, wrapped in a blanket. But it didn't look like anyone was questioning her—she'd yet to regain the ability to speak.

"Jason," Aria murmured, twisting her head. "Someone needs to—"

But someone already was. Apparently, the children weren't the only ones on campus that night. Several parents had been asked to chaperone the winter dance. And, in light of recent events, there had been several over-zealous volunteers...

"Jase!"

There was a flash of golden hair, then Gabriel was kneeling beside them.

It wasn't the first time the man had stumbled into a nightmare, and he wasted no time. One hand flew automatically to Aria, blindly checking her pulse whilst the other ripped open his son's tattered dress shirt, searching for the source of all the blood. What he saw confused him.

"This is the only place he's injured?" he murmured, glancing at Aria for the first time. "I don't understand. There shouldn't be so much blood."

The scratches running the length of Jason's body were ghastly, but no longer deep enough to place him in such peril. Of course, with the amount of blood he'd already lost...

"I healed him," Aria panted, trying to push up beside them. It was the first time she'd said it out loud. It was the first time she'd really registered it herself. "I mean, I tried..."

Gabriel's eyes flashed to her face, lingering there ever so briefly before he turned swiftly back to his son and lifted him gently off the blood-stained snow.

"That's what happened to you?" he asked briskly, ripping off his jacket and pressing it like a bandage to Jason's chest. "You don't have any injuries yourself?"

Aria sat up straighter, embarrassed to have split his focus. "Yes. I'm fine."

"What about your head?" he demanded, never taking his eyes off his son. "You're slurring."

It was impossible to hide anything from the man. She didn't know why she'd even tried.

"I cracked it on a rock, but that was ages ago. I really am fine."

Gabriel nodded once, but the second he'd seen both she and Lily were alert enough to be talking his mind had turned to other things. Years of living in a hellish prison beneath the ground had trained him well for such moments. His hands never shook, his confidence never faltered.

After waving away the on-scene medic, he proceeded to conduct the preliminary examination himself. Taking vitals, pulling back eyelids, running his hands over every inch skin to check for damage that may have gone previously unnoticed. Once he came to the inevitable conclusion that his teenage son had simply lost an extraordinary amount of blood he snapped his fingers like some imperial dictator, summoning the cowering medic back to his side.

"We'll have to do a transfusion. I'm O-negative. Universal donor. He can have mine."

The medic nodded swiftly, not daring to disagree. "If we can just get him to the infirmary—"

"Do it right now."

For a split second, Aria's famous uncle looked even more terrifying than the tiger. But on this point, even the trembling medic was unable to agree.

"Sir, I simply don't have the necessary equipment." He spoke quietly, but was firm at the same time. "Between that and the risk of infection—"

"Fine," Gabriel cut him off. "Get someone with a speed tatù to carry him." His eyes flashed impatiently around the clearing. "Where's Tristan—"

"It's a shame we don't have Benji," Catalina murmured, one of the only students to have remained in the clearing. "He must still be at the dance."

There was a beat of silence.

...holy smokes.

Aria froze in sudden horror, then turned to look at Lily. Their eyes met in the darkness as both girls came to the realization at the same time.

"Benji's not at the dance," Lily gasped, springing to her feet. "He was dragged away!"

The others flew into panic, but Gabriel went abruptly still.

"What do you mean?" he asked sharply. "What do you mean he was dragged away?"

At that very moment Luke swept into the clearing, having just corralled the rest of the students back to the dance. He didn't yet know what had happened in the woods, or which children were at the center of the drama. But a single look at his face said he should have guessed.

"Who was dragged away?" His skin paled a deathly shade of white as his eyes swept over the clearing, failing to see a particular face. "...where's Benji?"

Gabriel stood up slowly, still holding Jason in his arms. A silent look passed between him and Luke. Just a second later and they would have gone out together. But at that moment, the crowd of agents parted and two new people limped onto the scene. The older was sporting a strange array of cuts and bruises, while the younger was still clutching a large rock in his hands.

"We're back," Benji panted, raking back a curtain of messy hair. "Where's—"

There was a violent collision and he let out a painful gasp, struggling to breathe under the strength of his father's embrace. It lasted several suffocating seconds before Luke pulled away, shooting a quick look at James then taking his son by the upper arms.

"What happened?" he demanded, memorizing every scratch. Every smear of blood. "Tell me right now. Who did this to you?"

A sudden silence rang over the clearing. It was the question everyone had been waiting to ask. But Gabriel stepped in between them, still clutching his broken son in his arms.

"Later," he said shortly. "Ben, can you take him to the infirmary? *Quickly?*"

While Benji was clearly exhausted, he nodded immediately—paling slightly as his best friend was passed gently into his arms. Only then did he look up and see the others. Lily, still trembling in a blanket. Aria, half-kneeling on the icy ground.

"Is everyone..." He trailed off, feeling the first aftershocks of what had happened. "Are you guys okay—"

"Benji," Gabriel insisted.

"Right. Sorry."

He was gone in a flash, taking Jason with him. Gabriel followed without a second's thought, pausing only long enough to shoot Luke a parting glance. After so many years living as family, they no longer needed to speak. A single look would suffice.

Luke would stay with the children. Gabriel would look after his son.

The others stared silently towards the school as his silhouette grew smaller and smaller on the shadowy lawn. Benji and Jason had long since vanished, already safe in the infirmary, leaving the mess in the campus forest behind. And it was a *mess*.

Aria glanced about the clearing, taking in everything with a silent sweep of her eyes. It would be impossible to guess what had happened without including several small acts of God. The trees in a semi-circle around them had been scorched and blackened. The grass was long and wavy in some parts, while others had been frozen solid in a blanket of ice. Wide gashes had been carved right into the ground from the claws of the beasts they'd been battling. And *everywhere* was soaked in blood.

"Tell me what happened," Luke said quietly, as soon as the others were out of sight. The woods were coming to life around them, but for just a fleeting moment the four of them were alone. "How did Benji get those scratches? Why was Jason on the ground?"

Aria opened her mouth to answer, but found herself at a loss. Despite having lived through every excruciating second, a part of her mind still couldn't believe what had happened.

A school boy fight. Had a school boy fight really escalated into all of this?

"Did you recognize them?" Luke prompted softly, hyper-aware they were running out of time. "Did they say anything? Or was it someone you'd never seen?"

All at once Aria realized the reason for the agents, the reason half the school had emptied out onto the frosty lawn. It should have been obvious. She should have seen it from the start.

They think it's the same person who killed Professor Dorf.

She and Lily shared a panicked look, putting it together at the same time. James kept his opinion to himself. But he glanced nervously at his sister, waiting for her to take the lead.

"This isn't..."

She trailed off, staring over Luke's head to where Maize and Windall were rushing towards them. Both were already holding their weapons. Both were out for blood.

"What is this?" Lily asked shrilly, seeing the same thing. "Shoot on sight?"

Luke glanced behind him, then shook his head.

"Those are tranquilizers." But he glanced at the agents again before gently helping Aria to her feet. "Let's get you all inside. We can talk when your parents get here."

No sooner had he pulled her upright than James rushed to her other side—taking her silently away from his uncle and supporting her all by himself. She glanced at him in surprise, then gratefully accepted the assistance. Her strength was spent. She could barely take a step.

"Uncle Luke," she whispered. "This had nothing do with Dorf. This was just a fight."

Luke raised his eyebrows slightly, probably at the word *just*, but said nothing to contradict her. Instead, he nodded sharply then cocked his head towards the school.

"I need to speak with a few people. Wait for me just outside the trees. *Do not* go anywhere on your own; stay with the crowd of people. I'll be there in a moment to walk you inside."

The three friends obeyed silently, sticking close together as they moved through the milling crowd. For once, everyone's eyes weren't on them. The attack was still fresh. People were still scanning through the trees. For a moment, Aria was terrified what they might find.

"This feels wrong," she whispered to the others, watching as the agents divided into groups to search the rest of the grounds. "They don't even know what they're looking for—that it's a bunch of *students*, not some killer on the loose."

James said nothing, but Lily's face hardened.

"Is there a difference?" she asked coldly, staring out at the trees. "That psychopath could have killed Jason—murdered him right in front of our eyes. The bastard deserves everything that's coming to him. And it's coming...you can be sure of that."

A shiver ran across James' shoulders as the night played back in his mind.

"Do you think they'll find him?" he asked quietly, staring across the lawn. "He and the others, they just took off. But it's not like they could get through the gate."

Aria tested her weight gingerly, then leaned back into his arm.

"If he's smart, he'll have already shifted and gone back to the dance. But Lily's right—it's only a matter of time before they find him. The ground is covered in claw marks, and Jason..."

...Jason was clearly mauled by a wild beast.

She glanced suddenly towards the school, anxious to join him in the infirmary. At the same time, the ground tilted dizzily beneath her. A moment later, she found herself in the air.

"What are you doing?" she gasped, staring up at her little brother. For the very first time she could remember, the roles had reversed and he was carrying her in his arms.

He rolled his eyes with a blush. "You were falling over, klutz. What did you expect me to do?"

...let me fall?

At that moment, Luke returned—leaving a group of rather bewildered-looking agents in his wake. He didn't tell them what was said, but simply gestured up to the school. Halfway there, his phone buzzed with an incoming text. He glanced down at the screen, then let out a quiet sigh.

"Your parents have been delayed," he murmured. "They won't be here for another hour."

Aria and James shared a quick look.

"Why?" he asked. "What happened?"

Luke simply rubbed his eyes, walking tiredly across the lawn. "They're being held at the local precinct...reckless driving."

BY THE TIME THE OTHERS got to the infirmary, the transfusion had already happened. Jason was lying fast asleep on a hospital cot and Gabriel was sitting beside him—rolling his sleeve back down.

He glanced up when the door opened, then flashed a tight smile.

"He woke up as it happened, then fell back to sleep. The doctor says he'll be fine."

The friends paused in the doorway, letting out a collective sigh of relief before rushing to join them. Benji was sitting on the adjacent cot. But he was still wearing his clothes from the dance but, judging from the fact that he was also still bleeding, he hadn't allowed himself to be examined.

...yet.

"Put on a gown," Luke ordered, snapping his fingers at a pair of drawers. "I don't know why the doctor hasn't seen you yet, but that's about to be remedied."

Benji tensed immediately, registering the change of tone. His father had been a lot more indulgent when he thought his only child had been attacked by a serial killer. Now that he knew it was simply the latest in a long line of fights, that indulgence had lessened somewhat.

"I'm fine, Dad. There's no need to fuss—"

"*Benjamin.*"

"All right—fine."

He lifted himself off the cot, heading across the room to change. It probably would have been easier to argue his point if the bed where he'd been sitting hadn't been streaked in blood.

It's the sheets, Aria thought in a daze. *Why do hospitals have white sheets?*

"They'll be examining the three of you as well," Gabriel warned softly, keeping a hand on his son at all times. Unlike Luke, he was having a significantly easier time with things now that he'd seen Jason open his eyes. "Might as well get changed yourselves."

Aria's eyes flickered to the stack of gowns, but she gave them a wide berth—joining him by the cot instead. Lily was already there, sitting numbly on Jason's other side. As she reached out shyly to touch his hand, a pair of tears slipped down her face.

"None of that," Gabriel said gently, tucking back her ivory hair. "He's all right. And your dad will be here in a moment. Something about having to post bail?"

"That's my fault," Aria interjected. "Or at least—it's my parents' fault. Apparently, they decided now would be a great time to get arrested."

It wasn't the first time. The Wardells' driving habits were known throughout the county.

She perched on Benji's cot, staring down at Jason's face. There was something different about him, though she couldn't quite place it. It took a few seconds to realize what it was.

"...his hair."

While most of his tangled locks were matted with blood, there was a wave near the front that had somehow escaped the onslaught. Furthermore, it was no longer blond. It wasn't grey, it wasn't white. It was pure silver. Like someone had melted a star and dripped it onto his hair.

She reached out to touch it, then let her hand drop back to her side. "He's really going to be fine?"

Gabriel lifted his head, staring into her eyes. "Thanks to you."

She had no idea what to say in response. If anything, she felt unbelievably guilty. The fight had broken out over *her*. And she'd been knocked senseless before she could even manage to help.

"Trust me," she muttered, dropping her eyes, "it wasn't like that—"

At that moment, the door banged open and three new people swept inside. One headed straight for the cots, ignoring everything else. The others were just as anxious, but followed at what could best be described as a cautious distance.

"I'm sorry it took so long." Julian bypassed the others and embraced his daughter, shooting an angry look over her head. "I had to make an unscheduled stop along the way."

Rae pretended not to have heard while Devon blushed, muttering under his breath.

"I said I was sorry..."

The psychic ignored them, kissing his daughter's forehead before perching on the edge of Jason's bed. "Natasha and Molly will be here in a minute. How's he doing?"

Gabriel tightened his grip, eyes never leaving the boy's face. "He woke up for a few seconds, tried to say my name. The doctor says he'll be fine."

Julian flicked the silver hair with the hint of a smile. "He's going to love that."

Gabriel laughed softly. "I'm afraid he will."

"Which doctor was it?" Rae asked, coming up behind them. James was already tucked under one arm, while Aria was circled in another. "I could always check myself—"

"It was Porter," Gabriel answered. "He'll be fine."

She nodded, then spotted Benji in the corner. He'd headed obediently to the gowns under his father's watchful eye, but had yet to surrender completely and put one on.

"Come here, Benny. Let's get you cleaned up before your mother sees all that blood."

'Benny' was a privilege only Rae was allowed. One he 'despised', but secretly adored.

He pretended to scowl, but dropped the gown in a triumphant pile and headed back to the rest of them. Avoiding his father's disapproving gaze as he perched like a model patient on the bed.

Porter was good, but old-fashioned. Old-fashioned in that he still used things like high-tech equipment and modern medicine. Benji would much rather be healed supernaturally. Not only did it allow him to wear his own clothing, but it was over in the blink of an eye.

That being said, there was a bit more of an examination this time.

Luke must have texted that the children had been too over-whelmed yet to talk, because from the second Benji sat down Rae took matters into her own hands.

Without giving him time to respond, she took off his suit jacket under the guise of "seeing what we're dealing with," then sucked in a quick breath when she saw the scratches.

Unlike the children, who'd never done anything more than horse around with their fellow shifters, she and the others had been attacked many times before. At a single glance, she could tell you it was a large cat. And the list of active shifters with such a gift was few and far be-tween.

"It's not that bad," Benji said quickly, shifting uneasily on the cot. "The blood makes it look a lot worse than it is..." For once, the sudden spotlight didn't agree with him. "You should really be looking at Jase. He got it a lot worse than me."

It was quiet for a moment, then Devon stepped forward. "He got it a lot worse...from who? What happened tonight?"

The children froze in unison, shooting each other furtive looks.

It wasn't that they didn't want to tell—quite the opposite. It's just that they were dealing with stakes far higher than any they'd dealt with before.

Not only were students forbidden from using ink against each other on campus, but shifters were *never* allowed to attack in their animal form. Alexander could go to jail for what he'd done. And in the supernatural world, 'jail' didn't always come with what you'd call a fair trial.

He'll rot in a cell forever because of a high school fight? And his sister? And Eric?

Benji had been asked the question, but he lowered his head quickly—avoiding his uncle's eyes. When Luke stepped forward and lifted his chin, he let out a quiet sigh.

"It wasn't what you think. And I don't know how it got started."

...my turn.

Without having to ask, eight pairs of eyes shot to Aria. She blushed furiously and kept her own eyes on the cot—looping the questions again and again in her mind.

What will happen if I give Alexander's name? What will happen to Eric? To Sofia? Will they just be expelled, or will it be something worse? Did he even realize what he was doing—he looked out of his mind!

Then another thought interrupted. One that put all the others to rest.

He could have KILLED Jason.

Just like that, her decision was clear.

"Jason and I were walking to the dance," she began softly, "when all of a sudden, this—"

"—this shadow jumped out of the trees."

The others let out a gasp, then swarmed around the hospital cot as Jason's voice echoed off the walls. He was too weak to sit up, but his eyes were open. They bypassed the adults completely, burning with a searing intensity into each of his friends'.

"Hey." Gabriel leaned over him, taking the first real breath since he'd arrived. His eyes were shining, but his voice was steady and calm as he squeezed his son's hand. "Don't worry about that now. There are agents on the ground. We'll take care of it. In the meantime, you just rest—"

"No, we should settle this."

Jason hitched himself higher on the bed, biting his lip as scalding pain rippled down the center of his chest. The room was spinning in several directions, but he seemed determined to speak. In fact, there looked to be no stopping him.

"The whole thing was over in a second. It was dark, and whoever it was...they knocked us down before we could see anything that might help identify them now."

He paused ever so slightly before driving the point home.

"We have no idea who it was."

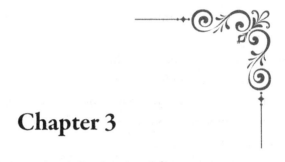

Chapter 3

When news had leaked out about the attack just an hour earlier, the parents had thought it was an open and shut case. They'd leapt into their cars and raced towards the school, under the impression that their children had been assaulted on the way to the dance by the same person responsible for killing the unfortunate professor. Speed limits had been broken, front doors had been left hanging open in the cold, but there was no question in their minds as to what had happened.

When Luke texted just a short while later, the plot had thickened. No, it was not a serial killer on the loose, but a regular fight. That being said, there was nothing regular about it. Laws had been broken. People had been mauled. And though he didn't yet know the identity of the attacker, the skirmish had raged on for quite some time. And there wasn't a doubt it would soon be revealed.

Their night of investigation turned into a mission of vengeance. Already they were scrolling through the lists of faculty and students, wondering who it would turn out to be. By the time they parked the car, they were already on to the next step in their heads. A quick stop in the infirmary to check on the children, then they'd apprehend and punish the wrong-doers themselves.

Under no circumstance had they considered there might be a third possibility. That the children would know what had happened...and lie.

Gabriel leaned back slowly, staring at his son without saying a word. As usual, it was difficult to know what he was thinking. But a single glance at his face said it wasn't something good.

The rest of them shot each other quick glances, not knowing how to proceed. Thrilled as they were to see the boy awake and talking, it certainly wasn't the answer they'd been expecting. And, needless to say, a sudden and seemingly deliberate gap in memory would simply not suffice.

The silence stretched on for ages before Julian broke it with a gentle voice.

"It must be difficult to remember...you lost a lot of blood."

The others latched on to this idea like a life raft. Of course the boy wasn't lying. He'd been almost bled dry right there on the forest floor. He couldn't possibly be expected to account for what had happened. Only his father remained unconvinced. And the rest of the children.

The second Jason made his declaration, they'd gone perfectly still.

While he might have been incapacitated, they didn't believe for a minute that he couldn't remember what happened. Especially not when they remembered every terrifying moment so well themselves. The fight between him and Alexander had been brewing long before the dance. Even if he couldn't recall the moment to moment, he surely knew who'd torn open his flesh.

What are you doing? Aria asked telepathically, trying to summon the ink she'd used before that allowed her to hear his unguarded thoughts. *Jason...we have to tell them.*

He didn't answer her, didn't even acknowledge he'd heard her speak. He kept his eyes trained on the others, drilling the message into them. Enforcing the silent command.

"Benji?" Luke prompted softly. The boy jumped in his skin, eyes jumping between his father and his friend. "You never lost consciousness and there were burns all over the trees. You clearly used your tatù and fought the thing. What was it? *Who* was it?"

All he wanted in the world was to answer. Three names were waiting, just on the tip of his tongue. But Jason met his gaze for a split second, and he swallowed them back.

"I...I don't..." He trailed off helplessly, not knowing what to say. "It happened so fast—"

"And when has speed been a problem for you?" Luke demanded sharply.

The room fell silent once more.

"Lily," Julian prompted softly. "Who was it?"

She froze like a deer in the headlights—looking more terrified than she had at any point in the evening when she was fighting the bear. Twice her eyes darted to Jason, but they came away blank. When she finally forced herself to look at her father, she could only stammer a request.

"Could we-could we maybe talk about it in the morning?"

Julian's lips parted as he stared down at her in shock. They shared a trust, the two of them. Even when she was a small child, Lily Decker had never looked him in the face and lied.

She hadn't exactly lied now, but that trust was clearly broken.

"I don't understand," Devon spoke loudly, shaking the room from its trance. "What the bloody— What is so difficult about this question? WHO attacked you? Tell us right now."

A ringing silence followed his demand. A silence he had no intention of honoring.

"James." He was standing in front of his son a moment later, startling him with the sudden proximity. "Tell me what happened. Who did this to your friends?"

The boy paled, glancing helplessly around the room.

"I have no powers," he deflected poorly. "I couldn't really see what was—"

"No, none of that," Devon interrupted impatiently. "I don't know why you're so hesitant to talk, but we know there was a fight. That's the reason we were called down, the reason one of you is lying on a hospital cot. A fight implies two sides, and the evidence is overwhelming. Some of you were clearly fighting back. Now *tell m*e who did this to you, before I lose what's left of my temper."

"There won't be repercussions, if that's what you're worried about." Rae took a step closer, eyeing the lot of them with motherly concern. "Whatever happened is over now. The second we have a name, that person will be removed from your lives forever. There's nothing to fear."

Devon nodded slowly, reaching out a hand. "James?"

The teenager flushed and stared down at his feet—not understanding he reason why he was being made to keep silent, but feeling Jason's piercing eyes just over his father's head.

"I got there late," he mumbled. "I couldn't tell you."

Rae made a sound of astonishment behind him, but Devon had already moved on. If his son wasn't willing to tell the truth, then he would demand it from his headstrong daughter instead.

"Arie."

Their eyes met, and she felt as though a dagger sank into her chest. The two had always been close, *impossibly* close, but the mission in New York had brought them to even greater levels of understanding. She understood what was at stake now. She understood why he was asking.

...but the answer wasn't hers to give.

She took a deep breath, watching as a line was drawn in the sand. Dividing two groups of people who should have been standing united.

We're going to regret this.

"It's like Jason said...we have no idea who attacked us."

FOR THE NEXT HOUR AND a half, the adults tried every trick under the sun to get their children to talk. From threats, to manipulation, to promises, to fits of blinding rage as they separated them into different rooms and proceeded to interrogate them from there.

Nothing worked.

They might not have known why they were keeping silent, but the friends had a pact of loyalty just as tight as their parents were bonded themselves. As long as Jason was insisting upon the story, they would honor it. Even if it brought with it a terrible price.

"I can't believe you're doing this," Devon muttered, taking his daughter back up the hall.

He'd walked with her down the length of the medical wing, hoping that a little distance from the others would help—only to be shut down the same way he'd been all evening. After twenty long minutes running into the same roadblocks as before, he'd decided to return to the others.

"You've done some crazy things at this school," he continued quietly. "Things that have made me reconsider sending you back the following year. But I thought you'd grown past it. After New York..." He gave her a fleeting look. "...I thought you'd changed."

Aria's face crumpled as a mountain of guilt threatened to crush her alive. She wished her mother had been the one to question her. The two of them shared the same fiery spirit. The same tactics, the same ploys. But her father? When he said things like that, she couldn't bear it.

"I'm sorry," she whispered.

He paused, glancing back at her. "I don't want you to be sorry. I want you to tell me what happened." He turned around to face her, standing just inches away. "Do you realize how serious this was? The extent of Jason's injuries? He could have *died*, Aria. There's a very good chance he would have if you hadn't managed to pull off that tatù. We would have spent the next few days planning a funeral—buried him over the weekend. And I guarantee that's not something Gabriel would decide to live through."

Each word stripped away another layer, leaving her raw and exposed.

"If you could just trust that—"

"Trust has to be earned," Devon said dismissively, setting off towards the infirmary once more. "Like I said...I thought you and I were past that."

BY THE TIME THE DOORS swung open the others were already back, scattered mutely around the room. A single look at their faces said they'd had just as hard a time as Aria had.

Lily was completely dejected, sitting between Natasha and Julian with a hollow expression on her face. James was off by himself, looking like he was going to be sick. While Benji was sitting perfectly still on the cot next to Jason's, the crook of his elbow was held tight in his mother's grasp.

There was a hitch in Aria's breathing when she saw her Aunt Molly. They'd yet to see each other—she and Natasha had arrived once Aria had already left. But while she had nothing but love and warmth towards the woman, she wasn't happy to see her now.

Quite the contrary, she found herself feeling borderline scared.

"I expect she didn't tell you anything," Molly snapped without ever taking her eyes off Benji's face. "This one couldn't tell the truth if his life depended on it."

Devon sank into a chair with a quiet sigh.

"No, she didn't."

Julian had prophesized as much. It was the reason he'd remained where he was, refusing to question his daughter further. The others had still felt compelled to try.

"Let me guess." She slipped off the cot, releasing Benji for the first time. "You just couldn't remember seeing anything? Too shocked? Everything happened too fast?"

Aria shot her aunt a helpless look, then lowered her eyes to the floor.

Ever since she was a child, Molly had been an ally. She was usually the first one the children went to when they got into trouble. Whether it was knocking down a prized lamp during a game of indoor baseball, or plotting the perfect revenge on an ex-boyfriend they'd sworn to hate. There was always a solution waiting for them. Always a hilarious greeting followed by a sunny smile.

But there were no smiles tonight. Molly had arrived at Guilder, to find her son's bloody evening jacket tossed in a pile on the floor. The others were tolerating the lack of compliance. *Barely*.

She was not.

"Answer me, Aria."

The words scalded the air as little angry sparks leapt from her fingers. Aria lifted her eyes, only to see her mother standing impassively by Molly's side. No, there were no allies tonight.

"Leave her alone," Benji muttered, keeping his eyes on the cot. "She doesn't know—"

Molly whirled around, absolutely incensed.

"Is that right!" she exclaimed. "Well, here's what *I* know. But there were scratches down the length of your body, wounds that couldn't possibly have been made by a man. It was a shifter. And, judging by the clearing, I seriously doubt there was only one."

Benji's eyes flickered up for the first time, staring at his mother in surprise.

"When did you see the clearing—"

"Do not change the subject, Benjamin!" she shouted. "The four of you are *lying* to us and I want to know why!"

"Did you start the fight?"

The room fell silent as everyone inside turned to look at Gabriel.

It was the first time he'd opened his mouth since Jason's sudden declaration. While the others had been arguing, he'd been thinking—quietly staring at his son's face.

"Is that what this is?" he continued softly. "You think it's better to get lectured by us than expelled from the school?"

Jason tensed in surprise, but kept quiet. It was the first time anyone had spoken to him directly since he woke up. They were keeping a respectful distance—in honor of him almost dying.

But that grace period had apparently worn off.

"I don't care if you started the fight," Gabriel said quietly. "And I don't care why you got into it in the first place. Whoever did this is *dangerous*. Are you going to leave such a person free to move about campus? In striking distance of your friends?"

Sometimes Aria wondered why the others bothered to interrogate people at all. Gabriel was clearly the best at it. Not only were he and his sister the least squeamish, but he always seemed to cut right to the core of the issue—letting everything else fall away.

She expected Jason to crumble. For him to be overwhelmed with guilt just like the rest of them. But instead he rose to the challenge with fire in his eyes.

"I don't know what to tell you...we have *no idea* who attacked us."

An audible hiss rose up from the parents, and the children cowered and cringed. Aria looked up just long enough to shoot Jason a glare, paired with a telepathic warning.

You had better have a bloody good reason for making us do this.

This time, he actually met her eyes. But before he could say anything Molly stepped into the middle of the room, throwing up her hands. "That's it—time for drastic action. Natasha?"

It took a moment to understand what she was implying. Then Jason bolted up on the bed.

"*No!*"

A memory tatù wasn't a casual thing to play with, and ink that delved into a subject's mind had a different set of rules than the rest. It would never be administered without consent.

That had never been a problem...until now.

"None of us is doing that," he said firmly, eyes flickering to his friends. "Not one."

This time, the shock of the refusal was much more pronounced. Several people started to speak at once, but it was Julian who knelt beside the bed.

"Why are you doing this?" he asked softly, eyes shining with concern. "Jase, if you won't tell us the name then tell us the problem. We can help—I promise we can."

Jason faltered for a split second, then shook his head firmly. In truth, he was having just as much trouble refusing their parents as the rest of them. But his mind had been made up since the moment they carried him, battered and bleeding, out of the trees.

"There's no need," he answered quietly, adding in a louder voice. "At any rate, there is no need for a tatù. We just never saw the person's face."

Julian leaned back with a hint of frustration as Gabriel leaned forward to take his place.

"A truth tatù, then."

They locked eyes for a split second before Jason shook his head with a sneer.

"Really?" he asked caustically. "Is that what you want?"

Lily and Aria exchanged an astonished glance as that inexplicable caginess spilled over with a hint of rage. He'd been polite and respectful to everyone else. But to his own father?

Whatever Gabriel was feeling, he was far too practiced to let it show. "I want you to be honest with me," he said quietly.

"Oh, like you're always honest with me?"

Aria's eyes squeezed shut as she brought a hand up to her temple.

I think I know what this is about...

Gabriel shook his head, looking utterly bewildered.

"What does that—"

But at that moment, the door burst open and the infirmary was flooded with light. A swarm of agents in the same dark clothing flooded towards them, moving with that terrifying synchronicity Aria had always found so comforting until now.

They were dragging something between them. She couldn't see what it was—only the occasional flailing of feet or broken gasp as they tried to stand on their own. Then all at once the procession stopped and a path cleared down the middle, revealing their prisoner.

Aria sucked in a breath.

They found him.

Alexander's face was dirty, there were scratches on his hands, and the clothes he was wearing weren't his own. Both arms were being held tightly by agents on either side—lowered to such a level that when they moved he lost balance completely and was simply dragged behind them. Now that they were stopped he struggled to get to his feet, panting silently in the sudden quiet.

"Of course," Luke muttered under his breath.

One of the agents stepped forward, acknowledging the adults with a nod of his head.

"We found him at the edge of the trees, trying to shift back." He spoke with brisk efficiency, as if this was a formal debriefing. Given the people he was addressing, that wasn't far off the mark. "I think he would have done it before, but he was trying to find someone else. There were other tracks on the lawn, but they vanished almost immediately. He's the only one we caught... So far."

Alexander wrestled silently against the hands holding him, but said not a word in his own defense. For a split second his gaze flickered up to Aria, then dropped back to the floor.

For the first time since arriving, Gabriel pushed off the infirmary bed—walking towards the prisoner with a dangerous calm. The sight of it was enough to freeze the entire room. A dozen pairs of eyes shot nervously to his hands. He stopped a few feet away, his eyes locked on the boy's face.

"What does he shift into?"

The agent glanced at Jason, noting the giant scratches torn down the center of his clothes, before clearing his throat. "...a tiger."

At that point, Natasha pushed to her feet. Of all the people gathered, she had a purely passive power and next to no combat experience. But that wasn't going to stop her. One look at the woman's face and she was ready to tear the shifter to pieces with her bare hands.

Julian put a steadying hand on her shoulder, though he looked exactly the same way.

What are you doing to do now?

Only Jason heard the question, echoing silently in his head. He glanced at Aria for a split second before anchoring his fists painfully against the mattress and swinging his feet to the floor.

"It wasn't him."

There was a mild explosion from the others as Gabriel whirled around, cursing in a language they didn't understand. That legendary calm vanished for a split second as he stared down at his son.

"How do you know, if you can't remember?"

When Jason stayed quiet, he turned back to the prisoner.

"Rae."

She nodded silently and moved forward, lifting her hands towards Alexander's face. But a second before she could touch him Jason stumbled forward, catching the back of her coat.

"You can't!" he insisted. "I'm saying it wasn't him. You have no right to think otherwise."

More to the point, she had no right to *do* otherwise.

The woman pulled in a steadying breath and turned around slowly, fixing him with a burning glare. At the same time, Alexander looked past her—staring at Jason in total shock.

"My daughter was in those trees, Jason." She spoke quietly, drilling in every word with the precision of a knife. "My own daughter...and you're saying it wasn't him?"

Jason's resolve faltered for a few wavering seconds. His eyes flickered again to Aria as he pulled in a shaking breath. Then those eyes flashed to Alexander, and he was once again in control.

"It wasn't him."

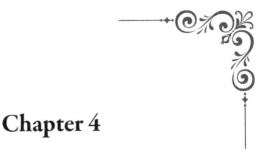

Chapter 4

C onsidering how long some parts of the night had dragged on, the next few steps flew past in the blink of an eye...

Alicia arrived and the infirmary was promptly emptied. She briefly examined the others, doing the cursory check for scrapes and bruises, finishing up with Jason. There was a golden glow and the marks on his chest vanished. A second later, he was turned out with the rest of them.

Around the same time, Tristan and Carter arrived back at Guilder. They'd been shamelessly avoiding the dance, dining together in the city, phones on silent. When they finally glanced down and saw the missed calls, they'd rushed to the parking lot so quickly they'd forgotten the check.

And finally...Alexander was released.

This was done with much more grumbling, but it was done nonetheless. With no evidence except the rapidly fading tracks in the clearing, along with five witnesses swearing to his innocence, there was simply no reason to hold him. No *technical* reason.

Of course, the others didn't go down without a fight.

"Where is he being housed?" Gabriel asked bluntly.

The doors to the infirmary had just closed behind them, and the entire processional was standing in the middle of the hall. Alexander lifted his eyes nervously, holding out both arms as PC agents removed a set of tatù inhibitors from his wrists. He hadn't said a word since being dragged out of the woods and into the infirmary. He certainly wasn't about to start now.

"He's in Joist," Carter answered. "With all the rest of them."

The words rang heavily in the silence that followed, implying a great deal more. With all the rest of them...like Jason, and Benji, and James.

The headmaster froze for a moment, thinking it over before quickly adding, "I can have him moved—"

"No, that's perfect. I can see Joist from my window," Gabriel interrupted softly, his eyes never leaving Alexander's face. "I'll be staying in the vacant cottage across the lawn."

It was certainly news to the rest of them, not least of all his wife, but never for a second was he challenged. Tristan graciously inclined his head before extracting a ring of keys from his pocket and pressing the correct one into Gabriel's hand.

"For as long as you need," he said simply.

"And what about the rest of them?" Molly asked loudly. It wasn't often she was on the losing side of a fight, and she could not *believe* they were being thwarted by their own children. "If this boy really is innocent, that means the real attacker is still out there."

Her voice practically blistered with sarcasm, and the friends flinched.

"That's true," Devon said slowly, watching each one in turn. "We'll need to have round the clock surveillance—agents patrolling every inch of the campus day and night."

Aria's mouth shot open to argue, but she held her tongue.

There had been an incident during her first year at Guilder—a fire in one of the faculty rooms that at first seemed accidental, but was later revealed to have been by design. Classes weren't cancelled, but the entire campus was on lockdown. Students were placed on strict curfew. Agents escorted them from class to class. There could be no deviance, no secrets. It was as though a giant magical microscope had been placed above them in the sky.

For a band of teenage trouble-makers...it was *hell*.

"I suppose we will," Carter said quietly, eyes flickering between Aria and James.

To say that he and Tristan had been shocked by their grandchildren's lack of compliance would be understating it to a massive degree. Given the bloody events of the night, both were tempted to simply bypass due process altogether and use a tatù to see the attack for themselves.

A single brush of Carter's hand and the truth would be revealed. All questions would be answered, and it was likely the subject would never even know.

But such a plan could never be admitted. And the children were keeping their distance.

"I'm sure that's not necessary—" James mumbled, but Benji nudged him silent.

The headmaster's eyes swept between the two of them, but he was too tired to argue the point. Half his staff was currently putting out lightning fires, and it was clear none of the friends was going to talk. Instead, he simply waved them off with a flick of his hands.

"We'll talk about this more later," he promised. "For now, you should get some sleep."

The words were meant for the parents just as much as the children. Maybe more. Like Molly, they weren't accustomed to defeat—let alone at the hands of their own. Neither were they accustomed to removing the handcuffs and letting the guilty party go free.

Gabriel's eyes burned as Alexander took a hesitant step away from them, rubbing his wrists.

"Don't go far," he said softly, offering the boy a terrifying smile. "I'd hate to have to track you down..."

"Alden," Tristan warned under his breath.

But the message had already been delivered. Alexander paled to the color of a living corpse as he nodded shortly and vanished into the darkness, glancing back only to give Jason a parting look.

There was a split second where Aria expected him to apologize. A split second where she half-expected him to turn back around. But their eyes met only for a moment.

A moment neither of them would ever forget.

HAD ARIA HARBORED EVEN the slightest hope of reconciliation with her parents, she would be disappointed. The second the family stepped outside, Rae and Devon splintered instantly from their children—walking in silence towards the adjacent parking lot.

"Where are you guys..." James caught himself quickly, trying not to act as shaken as he was. "Are you guys heading back to London?"

Devon kept walking as Rae turned back with a cold shrug.

"Nothing else we can do here." Her eyes flashed over to Joist Hall, where Alexander was just disappearing through the doors. "Besides, I don't think any of you is in danger. I also don't think all those agents forced to patrol the campus are going to find anything tonight."

Brother and sister shared a quick look, then Aria stepped forward.

"We're really sorry—"

"Rae," Devon interrupted quietly, tilting his head towards the lot. "It's late."

She turned on her heel without a glance at her children—heading across the shadowy lawn with her husband. They would keep up the cool façade until they reached the car. At that point he'd start yelling, she'd start hyperventilating, and both would demand that Julian keep an eye on their kids.

But the kids would never know that. They were left standing on the lawn.

"What the heck was that?" James muttered as they vanished into the night. He stared after them another moment before turning to his sister. "Why would Jason—"

"I don't know," she interrupted softly. When a strained silence fell between them, she looked him in the eye. "Really, James. I have no idea. But I'll find out. I promise."

He considered it a moment before nodding curtly and heading to the dorms. He'd only gone a step or two before she caught the back of his sleeve.

"And James...thanks."

He pulled himself free, looking back at her in surprise. "For what?"

She paused, glancing around to make sure they weren't being overheard. "For sticking with the rest of us. For keeping your mouth shut in there."

He stared at her a second longer before heading off into the dark. "They're my friends, too."

Yeah, she hung her head, feeling suddenly exhausted, *I guess they are.*

ARIA DIDN'T SEE ANYONE else on her way back to the dorms. The dance had been effectively cancelled, and the presence of agents had cleared the campus of any remaining students. She waited a while for Lily, milling around outside the steps of Aumbry Hall before deciding she must have missed her and heading inside.

The tower was dark and each step echoed off the high stone walls as she climbed slowly to the top floor. Most days, it seemed like a privilege—having earned a place right at the very top. But tonight she resented every jagged stair, dragging her feet up flight after flight.

By the time she got to her room, she was ready to pass out. A cursory glance showed that Catalina was clearly gone for the night—probably swooped back to the city by her parents. Now that she thought about it, there were probably going to be many students whose parents decided to pull them from class until further notice. It wasn't that much of a surprise.

First a dead teacher, now an attack at the winter dance? She plucked a few jeweled pins from her dark hair, letting them clatter to the floor. *It'll be a wonder if we have any students left at all—*

"Aria?"

She let out a little shriek, leaping back with a hand clamped to her chest. In her heavy-eyed delirium, she'd completely missed the fact that there was someone else in the room. A lovely girl in a sparkling dress, hovering nervously in the shadows.

...Sofia?

In a flash Aria streaked to the closet, banging a secret metal tile burrowed deep inside the wall. A second later a panel slid open, revealing an impressive cache of weapons underneath. She reached inside blindly, pulling out what unfortunately turned out to be a mace.

"Whoa!" The girl leapt back at once, lifting both hands in surrender. "Take it easy with that! I only came here to—"

"Get back!" Aria warned, waving it threateningly between them. "Get back or else I'll do what I should have done in those trees!"

Sofia paled, and nodded very slowly. "All right, I just—"

"What are you even doing here?" Aria demanded, unable to let the girl finish a single sentence. The adrenaline had spiked, and no matter how hard she tried to keep it together her ears were ringing with echoes of her friends' screams. "How did you get in!"

"The door was open," Sofia answered slowly, trying to temper the frantic speed of the conversation. "I knocked, then walked inside."

"And where's Caty?"

The girl paused a moment, then shook her head. "...who?"

Aria's fingers tightened on the grip, swinging the ancient weapon between them.

"My roommate," she snarled through clenched teeth. "Where is my roommate? Or do you expect me to believe she just magically vanished when you came inside?"

Sofia blanked, mind racing. "...she probably went home?"

The mace was lowered ever so slightly.

Yeah, I was thinking that myself...

With a vicious scowl, Aria dropped the weapon carelessly on her dresser—not noticing when it speared a hole right through the center of her biology homework. Now that the shock had worn off, any trace of fear had vanished with it. She was better than this shy, trembling girl. If it came to a fight, she didn't have a doubt as to who would win.

"What are you doing here?" she asked again, trying to project the same dangerous calm she'd seen her Uncle Gabriel speak with all night.

With him, it was highly effective. With her, slightly less.

"I just came to..." Sofia trailed off, looking suddenly off-balanced, as if she was asking the same question herself. "I wanted to apologize for what my brother did."

There was a beat of silence.

"You wanted to apologize...for your brother?" Aria repeated incredulously.

Sofia flushed, staring down at her shoes. "I know it isn't enough—"

"What about you?" Aria exclaimed, remembering the moment all too well when a second tiger leapt into the clearing. "You attacked Benji!"

"I *didn't* attack Benji—"

"You bit his arm!" she cried. "You dragged him through the trees!"

Just saying it made her blood boil in anger. She didn't know why she didn't fire up some lightning of her own and shock the girl right out the open window.

But Sofia took a step forward, eyes shining in the night.

"I didn't hurt Benji!" she insisted. "I was getting him away from Alexander! You saw what was happening, the guy was going to—"

She stopped herself quickly, looking terrified of what she'd almost said.

"...was going to kill him?" Aria finished softly. "Is that what you were going to say? That your psychotic brother was about to *kill* my best friend?"

It was like popping a balloon. There was a quiet gasp as Sofia deflated before her eyes. All that fiery insistence vanished, leaving her defeated and cold.

"I don't know," she whispered. "I don't know what he would have done."

Aria stared warily from across the room. It wasn't the answer she was expecting. Then again, Sofia was nothing like the other two. Eric was nothing but a surly enforcer, while Alexander...

"That's really what happened?" she asked quietly, wishing like mad she knew how to use her mother's truth tatù. "You were dragging Benji away from the fight?"

A silent sob shook the girl's shoulders. When she nodded, there were tears in her eyes.

"I'm so sorry about Jason," she gasped. "Please tell me he's all right."

It was in that moment that something very strange happened.

As Aria stood there, watching her start to cry, another voice started echoing through the room. One that sounded exactly like Sofia's, though the girl hadn't opened her mouth.

Tell me he's all right. Tell me Alex didn't really do it. Tell me my brother's not a murderer and we don't have to leave again. Tell me we can stay here. Tell me we can finally have a home—

She held up her hand, blinking quickly, unable to hear any more. When she lifted her head Sofia was staring at her strangely, not understanding what had just transpired.

"Jason's fine. They were able to heal him." She paused a moment before adding, "And he didn't give Alexander up. No one knows what really happened tonight."

Sofia froze where she stood, utterly stunned. Several times, she tried to think of something to say. But in the end, it was Aria who moved things forward—sinking down onto her mattress.

"I've got some questions, and I think you owe me some answers." She patted the space beside her, offering an olive branch at the same time. "We've got all night..."

Chapter 5

If you'd told Aria a few hours ago that she'd be sitting on her bed with Sofia Hastings, listening to her life story, she would never have believed you. To be honest, she'd probably have picked up the mace again and asked you to leave. But that's exactly what ended up happening.

"Just start at the beginning," Aria prompted gently, sensing the girl was at a bit of a loss.

"The beginning..." Sofia murmured, staring at the floor. "I guess our story actually begins the same way as yours does...with Jonathon Cromfield."

Aria blinked in surprise, sure she'd heard wrong.

"Cromfield," she repeated in confusion. "But how—"

"The battle helped bring your parents together, right?" Sofia interrupted softly. "Everyone knows the story. How they tracked down the hybrids, united the two agencies, turned both his top lieutenants against him. In a way, they'd have to thank him...for causing them to become so close."

"I guess..."

Sofia lowered her eyes with a look of extreme reluctance, as if she was dragging the next words from some hidden place deep inside.

"The battle brought my parents together, too, except...they were fighting on the other side."

This time, Aria was unable to hide her shock. She remembered questioning her parents about such a phenomenon just a few days before. The battle at the sugar factory had caused an enormous rift in the supernatural community—one so great that no single side could be eliminated completely. When the dust settled, they'd be assimilated back into the fold.

But she couldn't imagine it wouldn't come with certain restrictions.

Or conditions, she thought suddenly. *That's the word Alexander used...conditions.*

"So what happened?" she asked quietly. "They were arrested, or—"

"They weren't arrested," Sofia said shortly. "They were killed."

A hard silence fell between them. One neither girl was particularly equipped to break.

"There was an explosion," Sofia continued in monotone. "Something about a gas main blowing up behind a wall. Or at least that's what we were told later. The three of us were just babies at the time."

"The *three* of you—"

"Me, Alex, and Eric. We always joke that he's our cousin," she said dully. "Not quite part of the family, but close enough."

"That's funny," Aria said quietly. "That's exactly what my friends and I say, too."

Sofia smiled faintly, but it faded as her eyes drifted to the door. "If they knew I was telling you this..."

Aria tilted her head, catching the girl's eye. "What?" she quipped. "They'd rage out and try to rip us apart with their claws?"

There was a beat of silence.

"...too soon?"

Sofia laughed softly, breathing a bit easier for the first time.

"Anyway, there was a bunch of us children left behind to wait out the fight. As far as I know the three of us were some of the youngest, but I'm sure there were others. The plan was to keep us in a stronghold until the battle was over. Everyone talked about Cromfield like he was some kind of god. There wasn't any doubt that he would win."

She paused ever so slightly.

"That's probably why they didn't leave behind many guards..."

A clock ticked loudly on the wall behind them. A pair of songbirds cooed in the frosty night.

"The rest is just hearsay, but this is what I was told. Intelligence was shaky in those days, for both sides. When the PC sent agents to the stronghold, they didn't know it would be filled with children. They'd believed they were sent to eliminate the second wave of reinforcements instead. If they'd known, they probably wouldn't have..." She cleared her throat, trying to keep speaking in an even tone. "They weren't taking any chances with tatùs, so they ended the fight before it could even begin. Threw down a chemical agent to incapacitate anyone waiting on the other side."

Aria softly sucked in a breath, eyes filling with tears.

"Children aren't meant to survive such things," Sofia said softly. "Most of them didn't. The ones who did were very, very sick. It missed Eric and Alex. I wasn't so lucky."

Aria looked down at the bed, her mind spinning. Ever since they were children, she and the others had grown up hearing stories about the 'war'. When they were young enough, they used to act them out—playing the parts of their parents, waving their hands to shoot imaginary lightning bolts and waves of fire into the sky. But the stories they heard were always ones of valor. There was never any doubt as to which side was in the right and who the heroes of those stories were.

A rushed mission with faulty intelligence...and children died?

They'd never heard stories like that.

"But didn't they heal you?" Aria asked incredulously, thinking of Alicia's magic touch. "I mean...if you survived the initial blast weren't they able to fix whatever was wrong—"

"They can't," Sofia said briskly. "It did too much damage early on. But now that I'm older, it's at least tolerable. They give me injections to manage the symptoms and stuff."

Another silence fell between them.

"That day by the benches, when Benji asked if you were okay..."

The afternoon was just a blur, but she remembered Sofia's face quite clearly. It was as if the light inside her had gone out, leaving a lovely corpse standing in its wake.

The shifter nodded dismissively, well used to such things.

"It flares up when I'm tired, or stressed, or already sick."

"Tired or stressed, huh?" Aria's eyes flickered out the darkened window. "Two things you're bound to avoid at Guilder..."

Sofia bowed her head with the ghost of a smile. "It's a lot better than the alternative. I'm just thrilled that we're finally allowed to leave the Abbey. That we're finally allowed to attend an actual school."

The Abbey?

Aria's face clouded with a sudden frown.

"Wait...what are you talking about? The three of you couldn't have been living at the Abbey all this time. Ben and I practically grew up there—we've been inside every room. And even if you somehow were, they have a proper school—"

"The Abbey isn't just the monastery," Sofia interrupted. "Just like the Privy Council doesn't only exist on this campus. There are extensions all over Europe. Safe-houses. Sub-stations. Foreign offices. We were in a branch of the Abbey further north in England."

Aria's eyes widened in shock. She never knew. Then again, she'd never asked.

"A branch of the Abbey..." she repeated under her breath. "Like the one here?"

Sofia shook her head.

"It was an apartment complex. A series of apartment complexes, actually. Near Newcastle, but not too close to the ocean. It was still overseen by Commander Fodder..."

There was a note of deference in her voice. Whether you agreed with his politics or not, Anthony Fodder was a man who was impossible not to respect.

"He visited from time to time."

Aria shook her head slowly, trying to put it all straight.

The more she listened to the girl's story, the more a thousand little things were clicking into place. The way the three shifters recognized Luke, heeded his warnings not to make waves. The way Alexander had looked up sharply when Jason introduced himself—stressing the name Alden.

He must blame him. If Gabriel hadn't defected, there's a chance the battle could have gone the other way.

"So that's where you guys grew up?" she asked curiously, trying to recall if she'd ever been to Newcastle. "In this apartment complex?"

For the second time Sofia shook her head.

"I wish it had been that simple, but we bounced around a lot. After the exposure I was always sick, and the regular places they used didn't always have the things we'd need." She paused, wondering whether to continue. "By the time we got older, I was no longer the problem."

Aria stared at her for a long moment.

"Alexander?"

The girl sighed, trying to think of a way to explain her older brother.

"He hated that we moved so much, that we were shuffled from place to place. It didn't take long to figure out we weren't exactly welcome in the supernatural community, and he resented it. He started getting into fights, started trying to get thrown out. They were considering settling us somewhere in Scotland when the commander summoned us to the actual Abbey for a meeting."

She paused again, eyes glassing over as she remembered.

"It was...a little intense. He sat the three of us down in his office, then started reading off our rap sheet. Alex's rap sheet more like it. He spoke slowly, and it took forever. By the time he was finally finished, there wasn't a point left to be made. We'd blown it. Burned one too many bridges."

Aria shook her head, trying to imagine. She knew Benji's grand-father almost as well as she knew her own. And, while she loved him dearly, there was no one better at giving a lecture.

"So what happened?"

Sofia lifted her head suddenly, like she'd been thinking of some-thing else.

"We were wrong," she said simply. "He wasn't kicking us out for good; it was exactly the opposite. He told us the fall term was just start-ing at Guilder, offered us a place at the school. When Alexander asked why, he got really serious and said that every great accomplishment is built on a mountain of failures. He said what happened in that bunker was the worst of those failures, and that the system had been failing us ever since. He said it was up to us to turn things around. Said that this was our chance at a better future, and he'd help us in whatever way he could."

By the end of the story, she was smiling. A lovely, hopeful smile that seemed to brighten everything around her. But as she glanced out the window, that smile went suddenly cold.

"...and then tonight happened."

Aria dropped her eyes to the bed, feeling a little cold herself.

Yeah... tonight.

It was quiet for a long time, considering they were virtual strangers. Yet somehow there was nothing uncomfortable about it. Both were merely sitting there, completely lost in thought.

After a few minutes, Sofia ventured a shy question of her own.

"Why did Jason keep quiet about what happened?"

Aria lifted her head slowly, surprised to find that she was intensely relieved that he had. Of course, there was no way for him to have guessed their story. Of course, considering the tiger almost mauled him to death, their story was no excuse. And yet it managed to change things.

"I don't know," she said honestly. "We all wanted him to. I thought our parents were going to explode, but...he didn't say anything. He wouldn't let us say anything either."

Sofia stared a moment, then nodded quickly—looking back down at her hands. "...thank you."

Aria's eyes narrowed as a good deal of that relief faded away. "Don't thank me—I would have done it." She glanced ever so briefly at the smears of blood staining her glittering dress. "I don't care how crappy a hand he was dealt, your brother still almost *killed* someone today. It started as a stupid argument and almost ended a man's *life*."

Sofia's breath caught in her throat as she pushed to her feet.

"I know," she said quietly. "Trust me—I know."

Aria eyed her sharply, refusing to let her off the hook.

"Has he ever done something like this before? You said he got into fights—"

"*Fist*-fights," Sofia said earnestly. "And they were nothing like this. I couldn't believe what I was seeing tonight. The fact that he actually shifted..."

Her eyes filled with tears and she turned quickly to the window.

"Anyway, I just...I just came here to make sure Jason was okay. And to say I'm sorry."

Aria pushed to her feet as well. Strangely enough, the night had raised far more questions than answers. But one thing was clear: This girl, at least, had nothing to apologize for.

If she was being honest with herself, Sofia Hastings was actually rather sweet.

"I'll pass that along."

They locked eyes for a split second before Sofia nodded and headed to the door. Her hand was already on the knob when she glanced back around.

"About Benji, I would never..." She trailed off, dropping her eyes to the floor. "He's the only person who's been nice to me since we got here. I'd never hurt him, Aria."

A strange mix of emotions stirred in Aria's chest. She shrugged dismissively.

"Yeah, well...he's nice. It doesn't mean anything."

Sofia's lips parted with a hint of surprise, then she nodded quickly and vanished into the darkened hall. Aria stared after her for a long time before shutting the door with a telekinetic flick of her fingers. It clicked shut as she sank onto the bed, staring up at the ceiling.

Something hard crunched beneath her. She shifted around to find the broken pieces of a crown. They glittered in her open hand, like tiny shards of ice.

...long live the queen.

Chapter 6

"**S**he's so quiet when she sleeps...like an entirely different person."

The curtain of dreams fell away as Aria's mind slowly awakened, too groggy to latch on to the disembodied voices talking casually above her.

"I thought of that. Once, during our freshman year, I drugged her with some of that tea we found at Aunt Angel's. Thought we might get along better if she was unconscious most of the time."

"What happened?"

"She woke up halfway through and smashed the teapot over my head."

Aria's eyes fluttered open to see Benji and Lily sitting on her bed—shoes kicked to the floor, sipping cups of espresso. The sun was up and they'd already drawn the curtains. Of course, they didn't bother waking her. They were merely chatting, leaning against the headboard on either side.

"Get off my bed."

They glanced down with twin smiles, pleased she'd decided to join them. Another cup of coffee appeared and was pressed into her hand. The mace Benji had been swinging dropped casually to the floor.

"Good morning!" he said cheerfully, looking much better once he'd had a chance to sleep off the events of the previous night. "You certainly took your time waking up."

Aria glared up at him, wincing against the halo of sunlight. "How did you get in here? There are rules, you know—"

"I climbed up the tower."

She and Lily glanced out the window with the same dubious expression. They wouldn't put many things past their charismatic friend, but it was a hundred-foot drop down slick stone.

His smile faltered, then turned into a scowl. "Fine. I came in through the front door. Elpis is at a staff meeting with the rest of them."

A staff meeting.

"You think it's about us?" Aria asked quickly. The last remnants of sleep had vanished with the first sip of coffee, and she was putting things together a lot faster now. "The meeting?"

Benji shrugged, glancing away as she checked to make sure she was still fully clothed.

"They usually are."

Sure enough, the dress had survived an evening of restless sleep. Though it certainly wasn't in the same condition as when Molly had hung it so proudly in her closet.

"I think it's bad luck to fall asleep in a bloody ball gown," Lily observed, glancing down at the crimson splashes across the jewels. "Wasn't that the secret lesson of Cinderella?"

When Julian had brought home a book of fairytales for his young daughter, his wife had countered by purchasing her the Grimm tales upon which they were based. As a result Lily had a whimsical, if slightly twisted, view on most parts of the world.

"Marie Antoinette," Benji corrected authoritatively. He stirred another lump of sugar into his coffee with a shimmering stick Aria recognized as a part of her deceased tiara. When he caught her looking, he tossed it onto the shelf. "You know, you're supposed to *wear* these—not break them."

"I'll keep that in mind," she grumbled, shoving him off her comforter. "Well, if there's a staff meeting, I'm assuming everything's cancelled because of last night?"

"Just the morning," Lily answered. "They shifted the schedule to make up for time lost to the dance, and we still have classes in the afternoon."

Aria nodded briskly, opening her closet with a flick of her fingers and levitating herself a robe. "So if you're here already, then where's—"

Before she could finish her question, the door burst open and a handsome man stood in the frame. He took one look at the strange scene in front of him before storming angrily inside.

"Why didn't you wait for me?"

The girls lifted their eyebrows while Benji pushed abruptly to his feet, setting down his cup of coffee. "Why didn't I *wait* for you?" he repeated sharply.

Jason stopped mid-stride, looking instantly repentant. "On second thought, it's completely understandable—"

"Good," Benji interrupted, blistering with sarcasm. "I'd *hate* to have inconvenienced you."

Jason bit down on his lip, edging discreetly to the far wall whilst keeping a careful eye on his friend's sparking hands. "You never told me what your dad said to you last night." His voice dropped to half volume, speaking almost to himself. "You didn't say much of anything..."

Stupid, stupid, stupid.

The girls exchanged a quick look, then settled back for what promised to be a show.

"Oh, I'm sorry," Benji snarked, raising his eyebrows in mock innocence, "did *you* have a question?"

"Ben—"

"You wanted to know what exactly my dad said between threats of dismemberment and charges of obstruction of justice?"

Jason flushed, wondering why he'd chosen to speak. "Actually, we can just talk about it later..."

But Benji was on the warpath. He swiftly crossed the room, coming to a sudden stop at his best friend's side.

"You see, Jase, I'd *love* to answer...but every time I try to remember what happened it's like this strange fog comes over me and I just can't seem to manage."

If there wasn't a chance the argument would end in blood, Aria might have smiled. The boys played rough. But Jason clearly didn't have a leg to stand on, and Benji was just getting warmed up.

"Look, guys, I'm really sorry—"

"Have you ever had something like that happen?" Benji continued, unaware his eyes were flashing electric blue. "Where someone asks you a simple question, but you can't seem to *freakin' answer*?"

Jason nodded quickly, bowing his head. "I get it, all right? And I'm really—"

"On that note, are you feeling better?"

The conversation screeched to a halt as Jason lifted his head, thrown by the sudden shift in direction. "Uh...yeah. Alicia completely healed me."

Benji nodded briskly. "Good."

A bolt of lightning flashed between them, and Jason flew into the wall. There was a painful groan as he slid slowly to the floor, regretting the moment he'd decided to get out of bed.

"Careful not to land on the mace," Lily said lightly.

He pushed to his feet, then stepped back quickly to avoid the serrated spikes.

"Was this intended for me?" he asked warily, giving it a bizarrely practiced twirl before putting it back in the cache. "Or did you just have a busy night?"

"Busy night," Aria replied. "Your friend Sofia paid me a visit."

Benji looked up immediately, every ounce of humor fading from his face. "Why—is she okay?"

The girls shared another secret glance and Aria fought to control a smile.

"She's fine. But, given the fact that she attacked us then snuck into my dorm room, I want to thank you for asking if *she's* okay."

Benji nodded distractedly, missing the finer points. "But she's really all right?"

Aria softened in spite of herself, remembering their words from last night. Yes, Benji was kind. And he forgave too quickly. Though she couldn't help but think this was a little different.

"She was worried whether Jason had come out of it," she began slowly. "And she was very insistent about you. She said she didn't attack you. That she just dragged you away from the fight."

Benji turned his gaze to the window, looking uncharacteristically thoughtful. "That's true. She had me by the arm, but it didn't hurt. The second we left the clearing, she let me go and just stood there. I kept waiting for her to attack, but...nothing. I finally tried to go back, but every time I started to run past her she'd get in my way. By the time James got there, the other students must have heard what was happening. They flooded into the trees, then she was just gone. I was hoping she'd shifted back into herself," he murmured. "You know, before..."

Aria turned from one boy to the other.

"...before she got caught like Alexander and dragged into the infirmary?"

"Only to be cleared," Lily added quickly. "Don't forget that part."

Jason's cheeks flushed. "Yeah, about that..."

FOR THE NEXT HALF-HOUR, three of the friends took turns berating the fourth.

There was everything from ranting, to hissing, to shouting, to enough electrical shocks that it began to seriously set back the good doctor's work.

Strangely enough, it was Lily who was the most effective. Since they were children the girl had been like a little sister, and when she spoke of lying to her father there were tears in her eyes.

By the time they were finished, Jason looked like he'd rather have gone another few rounds with the tiger. But he was no less firm in his resolve.

"I'm sorry." He said it only once, but he meant it with all his heart. "But we *can't* tell them."

"Why in the bloody—why not?!" Benji demanded. "And don't think you're the one taking the heat on this one! If anything, they're going easy on you after your little tiger attack!"

...little tiger attack?

Jason bowed his head, absorbing each new barb with quiet patience. He hadn't said a word while they'd been venting, hadn't done a thing to defend himself.

But on this point he was perfectly clear.

"I know that," he said softly. "But what do you think will happen if we tell them? The guy shifted, then attacked us. He's eighteen. They won't just kick him out of school—he'll go to jail!"

"And you care about that?" Lily asked incredulously. "The guy was about two seconds away from *murder*, Jason. Maybe he *should* go to jail. Before something like this happens again."

"That can't be your real reason." Aria said softly, searching his eyes. "Alexander's punishment would depend entirely upon what information you gave them. You know perfectly well how to tone things down and help him avoid prison. You don't want him gone. You want him to stay."

Jason glanced at her swiftly, then turned his eyes away.

"If that's the case, you think it's enough that he gets expelled?" he countered. "Like this was some...some academic infraction?"

"So what then?" Benji demanded. "You think jail is too much and expulsion is too little. Do you know where that lands him?" He pointed out the window to Joist. "Right here. Like nothing ever happened. Meanwhile, we're the ones getting crucified by our parents on the south lawn."

"I will fix things with our parents," Jason swore. "I don't know how yet, but I'll figure out a way. You have my word."

Lily folded her arms tightly across her chest. "And in the meantime?"

He flashed a tentative smile, trying to coax one back. "In the meantime, we'll keep an eye on things ourselves. Decide how *we* want to handle it."

She bit down on her lip, refusing to be swayed. "Tell me that's not what this is about. Some schoolboy need to take control of the situation so you can dole out your own punishment. This is no time for revenge, Jase. He almost *killed* you."

"And I won't forget it," Jason replied lightly. "But before we go any further, I must caffeinate. You can hardly expect me to fend you guys off in my present state."

A hard silence fell over the room.

"I was recently attacked by a *tiger*, you know..."

This time, it was harder not to smile.

Last night the lights had been dimmed, the crowd had been shouting, and the smell of fresh blood had saturated the infirmary. Things looked about as bleak as they could get. But that morning, in the fresh sunshine drenched in the smell of espresso, they looked significantly brighter.

Benji and Aria exchanged a quick look before he rolled his eyes and clapped Jason on the back with a grin. Shocking him once more for good measure.

"Come on, let's get our stuff and go down to breakfast. You're buying."

Lily snorted under her breath, sweeping past them. "You're buying for the rest of the semester."

Jason grinned, letting them pass before glancing back once it was just him and Aria. "I wanted to thank you," he said softly, remembering that moment of golden light filtering through the trees. "I don't know how you did it...but you saved my life."

What else does he remember? she thought suddenly. *Does he remember what we were talking about before it happened? How we decided to make things official? Make a proper go of it?*

She stared at him for a moment, then decided he did not.

"You can thank me by not throwing it away."

His smile faded slightly and he gave a quick nod. She'd have to change out of the ball gown before meeting them for breakfast, but she caught him at the last moment by the sleeve.

"Jason...please tell me why."

He could deflect with the others if he wanted, but she'd been there from the beginning. She'd seen it happen from start to finish, the whole bloody affair. The guy was fair, but he was his father's son through and through. Actions deserved consequences. There was no way he'd just let this go.

He paused for a suspended moment, glancing to make sure the others had gone. Then he lowered his voice and turned back to her, staring deep into her eyes.

"The guy's an orphan with no friends, limited family, and an incredibly tenuous position at this school. The one girl he wants is the one he can't have, and he just placed himself in the hands of the only guy standing in his way. He's reckless, impetuous, and a breath away from self-destruction."

The hint of a smile played at the corner of his lips.

"What's the worst thing you can do to someone like that?"

Aria knew the words without him even saying them. Like she'd pulled them out of his head.

Forgive him.

Jason flashed a quick smile and swung the door shut behind him. Leaving her standing alone in her room, silently wondering at the intricacies of the human mind.

Forgive the man, and he can never pay you back. Forgive him, and a part of his life is forever forfeit. It's not a fight he can win. It's not a debt he can pay. It is the death blow.

Unless he manages to change the game...

"HE'S NOT GOING TO BE in class," Lily said for the tenth time, walking arm in arm with Jason like some kind of ballerina-turned-attack-dog. "There's *no way* he'll be in class."

"Even if he is—it's fine." Jason continued humoring her with a patient smile, allowing himself to be escorted even when her own class was gathering on the opposite side of campus.

"It's not like he's going to try anything," Benji muttered. "Not with your dad staying in a cottage on the other side of the lawn. I'd be surprised if he isn't playing sick."

Aria said nothing as they made their way through the corridors. Unlike the others, she hadn't taken part in the riveting discussion that had started at breakfast. She kept her eyes on her porridge, occasionally waving away curious students who came to glean scraps of juicy information by hovering too close. It wasn't that she wasn't interested, there was just simply too much going on in her head to focus on any particular thing. That being said, she didn't agree with her friends' assessment.

Alexander Hastings wasn't the type to play sick.

"That's right," Lily said brightly. "I'd almost completely forgotten about Uncle Gabriel. He'd be a fool to show up today. There's just no way he's going to be in—"

The friends stopped outside the open door.

"—class."

There were still a few minutes until the bell, but the room was already bustling. Nothing sparked student attendance like a new campus scandal, and this was one for the books. The buzz of whispered voices was so loud, Aria was surprised she hadn't heard it down the hall.

And there, sitting in the middle of it all, was Alexander Hastings. He was flanked by Sofia and Eric, both of whom froze the second they walked inside.

A momentary lull fell over the room as the two sides stared each other down. It hadn't been confirmed, of course, that the shifter was the person responsible. The only thing people knew for certain was that he'd been called in for questioning after a fight in the woods.

But the open animosity between him and Jason was already more than enough to keep the rumors going, and the tension radiating between them now was doing nothing to help.

You wanted him here, right? Aria asked telepathically, startling Jason from his trance. *This was your decision. So go to your seat. Everyone's watching.*

He pulled in a quick breath, squared his shoulders, then breezed straight through the desks to his chair in the back of the room. The crowd parted before him like a knife through butter. The only thing that made it slightly difficult was the fact that Lily was still clinging to his arm.

"Kind of cramping my style here, Decker."

She completely ignored him, glaring Alexander down as they walked past his desk. For once the guy didn't make eye contact, but that only seemed to infuriate her even more. By the time they got to the back of the room, she was considering lighting his desk on fire.

"Just because you've resolved to take the high road doesn't mean I have to." She spoke softly enough to keep out the rest of the class, but loud enough for the shifter to easily hear. "I pulled a few helpful tips from my mom's old interrogation files that might do him some good.

Just give me a hair dryer and a nail file, and we'll see how long he manages to—"

"Miss Decker! What a surprise!"

The class looked up with a start as Dorian Locke breezed into the room, nodding a cursory welcome to his students. His eyes swept over the room once, taking in every detail, before falling on the fledgling psychic with a little smile.

"Aren't they missing you in advanced calculus?"

Her jaw tightened as she glared holes in the back of Alexander's head, then she forced her face into a polite smile. "I suppose they are. I'll see you *right* after class, Jase. I'll wait in the hall."

Jason's eyes twinkled with amusement. "Thanks, Mom."

She swatted the back of his head and headed back through the desks, hovering uneasily in the doorway before accidentally catching Dorian's eye and vanishing with a tight smile. The second the door closed behind her the room fell quiet.

"This is a nice change," Dorian joked, setting down his bag. "It's usually all I can do to get you all to stop talking..."

There were no smiles, no laughter. Nothing but creepily attentive eyes. He paused mid-step, looking them over before taking off his glasses with a quiet sigh.

"Well, I suppose you've all heard, so there's no point in beating around the bush. We had a bit of exciting news the other night, and I'm afraid it concerns someone in this very room."

Aria stiffened in her chair, staring at him in shock. Surely he wouldn't go into it in front of the class. Didn't a faculty meeting imply the teachers had been sworn to secrecy?

In the seat next to her, Jason had gone perfectly rigid. Just a few seats ahead of him Alexander sank a few inches lower in his chair, gripping a pencil so hard it had begun to break.

But the rest of the class was spellbound, staring with wide, unblinking eyes.

"No point putting it off any longer...let's have a round of applause for our Winter Queen!"

It was dead quiet.

Then the entire class burst into laughter.

Aria let out a breath of relief, shooting a quick glance at Jason before rising to her feet with an overly-theatrical bow. The class laughed louder, bursting into applause as she sank back into her chair. Dorian was watching her from the front of the room. Their eyes met for a brief moment and he inclined his head with the faintest of smiles. Her cheeks flamed as she grinned in return.

When it finally quieted down, he got to business—collecting old papers, assigning reading, generally doing whatever teachers did to keep busy when armed with the knowledge that one of their students had recently tried to rip another in half. They'd made it through a good fifteen minutes without anything too terrible happening when, all at once, that luck came to an end.

"—which brings us to everyone's favorite subject: research papers!"

The class let out a collective groan, wishing very much that he'd forgotten. But Dorian refused to be daunted, perching on the edge of his desk with that signature enthusiasm.

"Now, none of that! Listen, this isn't your average term paper. I'm not demanding that you pick some old dead person or an ancient war. This year, we're going to be asking questions."

"Questions?" Milo repeated incredulously. "What do you mean?"

Dorian smiled, leaning against the desk.

"If I asked you to write me a paper on Napoleon, all it would prove is that you know how to cut and paste things off the internet. You'd be wasting my time and yours. Instead, I want you to think of some burning question, a bit of cognitive dissonance that's never gone away...and write about that."

The class stared back at him in confusion.

"You mean, some question we've always had about history?" Lindsey asked. "Like why some explorer sailed to this place instead of that?"

"What am I always telling you?" Dorian answered. "We're making history each and every day. It's been brought to my attention that these papers of yours usually involve the history of this school. You select a prominent figure and make a report. This isn't going to be much different, except we're going to be dealing with very modern history. The things happening right now."

Aria leaned back in her chair, thinking it over. While she had plenty of questions about the running of the school, she wouldn't have thought many of them to be appropriate. Then again, it was an interesting suggestion...several things leapt immediately to the front of her mind.

"Like, why did we decide to integrate with the Abbey?" a shifter near the front asked. "Why it took so long for women to be allowed into the school?"

Dorian snapped his fingers with a smile. "That's exactly it! Pick a question and start from the beginning. Research both sides of the argument. Who stood for what? What was the determining factor? You're all going to be expected to participate in this government one day. It will help you greatly to understand how it works."

Benji cast Aria a sideways look, fighting back a grin. Free rein to dig into the sometimes-shady past of the Privy Council? It was a dream come true.

But a dream that came with a catch.

"To make things easier and gain a dual perspective, we're going to be doing this paper in pairs," Dorian continued, raising his voice to make himself heard. "Choose whoever you like, then spend the rest of class coming up with a question. Have it on my desk by the time the bell rings."

It should have been simple. They'd done multiple projects in pairs before. But at that moment, the class came together in one of those rare moments and decided to do something cruel.

Like clockwork, one person turned to another—pairing off so strategically and quickly, that by the time the friends saw it happening it was already done.

In the end, there were only three people left. A natural pair, and the odd man out who demanded placement all the same. Aria closed her eyes with a sigh. She should have seen it coming.

"Milo and Henry," Dorian murmured, moving down the rows and scribbling names down on a clipboard. "Maddox and Trisha, and...and the three of you."

He stopped where he stood, staring down at them in surprise.

"I'm sorry...I wasn't expecting that."

Aria sank a few inches lower in her chair, glaring fiercely at whichever students peeked around to see if their plan had worked. No one was brave enough to look at her directly, but the result was the same. She, Jason, and Alexander would be writing a research paper together.

And let the games begin...

Chapter 7

Dead. Quiet.

The rest of the class was busy working—rather, they were busy gossiping about what might be happening in the back of the room and laughing under their breath. But the three desks pushed against the far wall were dead quiet. The people sitting in them were statues. No one took a breath.

Bloody perfect.

Aria's eyes flickered over Alexander's shoulder, scanning the room for the familiar splash of red hair. Usually, she could count on Benji to save her from things like this. Usually, it would have been implied. But today, she was shocked to see that he might need some saving of his own.

Not only had he been sequestered off to the opposite wall, but he was sitting with the most unlikely of partners. Even with her back turned, Aria recognized the glossy sheet of espresso hair.

Her eyes narrowed as the two friends locked eyes.

Traitor.

He didn't need saving after all. He was perfectly content with his choice of partner, even if she had recently dragged him across campus disguised as a jungle cat.

"This doesn't need to happen," Alexander said quietly, pushing back his chair. Aria looked up in surprise to see his eyes glued to the desk. "I'll ask Locke if I can just do it on my own."

A retreat if ever she'd seen one. Only, there was nothing of sur-render in the way Alexander was speaking. It was more like he simply didn't know what to do. His skin was flushed, his hands were trem-bling, and he had the same manic expression as that first moment Jason had cleared his name.

"He won't let you," Jason said shortly. He was casually avoiding eye contact himself, tracing the edge of his notebook. "And even if he did, it's not like he could explain why if anyone asked."

The shifter pulled in a breath, trying to keep steady. "You two pick something, then. I'm cool with whatever you want."

Another retreat. This one was even more noncommittal than the first.

Aria glanced between them for a moment, then lowered her gaze. Yes—this was going to be excruciating. But since they'd been given no other option, the best thing to do would be to hunker down and get through it as quickly as possible.

Her mind raced as she tried to come up with a suitable question. There were so many to choose from, but in the context of a school pa-per that list shrank dramatically. The first question was the most ob-vious—one she was sure both Benji and Jason had already thought of themselves.

How were their parents able to defeat Vivian? What secret weapon tipped the scales?

Since they were children, they'd been asking the question. Ever since they heard the story about the day the skies of London rained down fire and ash. There were so many accounts, they'd been able to glean a wealth of information. From random agents, to old alumni, to the occasional case report that hadn't been redacted beyond belief.

Their grandparents had quartered off the city, standing like unmov-able sentries at each major point of entry. Their parents had led the charge, scaling the sides of buildings and racing down the streets. For the first and only time in history, powers were used out in the open. The two worlds had blended together, one uniting to save the other from ruin and death.

And *that* is where everything got murky.

Because amid the heat of the battle, their parents suddenly left. Because when Vivian's forces rallied, they returned by themselves to the waterfront to make a final stand.

There was no way they could have defeated her. Even with all of them standing together, they were so outnumbered there was simply no way they could have survived. And yet...they won.

Their kids asked a thousand times, a thousand ways. From yelling, to sneaking, to bargaining, to flat-out begging to be told the answer. But on that solitary point, their parents wouldn't budge.

And since they were the only ones who'd been present, the secret was theirs alone to keep.

Yes, *that* was the question Aria wanted to ask. But it was a question without an answer.

"Ah, come on. You must have questions about this place." Jason lifted his head suddenly, looking at Alexander for the first time. "After all, you just got here."

The shifter's lips parted, but he could think of nothing to say. One hand was gripping the spokes of his desk. Tiny pieces of metal had started to chip away.

"Let's just do something basic," Aria muttered, levitating a pencil out of her bag. "What about the fire? There has to be something there—"

"What about security?" Alexander interrupted, recovering his stride. "This is supposed to be one of the safest places on earth. What about asking how someone was able to get away with murdering a teacher in the middle of the night?"

A shocked silence fell over the desks as he leveled Jason with a hard stare.

"I know you think I did it."

The pencil snapped in Aria's fingers, but Jason held his gaze without a trace of fear.

"Would that be so unlikely?" he asked softly. "We all know what you're capable of."

Not good, not good, not good!

Aria's eyes flickered across the room to Dorian, but he was leaning back in his chair—legs perched on the desk as he studied a book in his lap with a faint frown. While there were several other people secretly watching, none of them wanted to help. Quite the contrary, the mystery of what transpired the night of the dance had reached critical levels, and they were eager for something to break. That left Benji...who was bent over his paper, oblivious to the world around him.

Short on allies, Aria turned to Jason herself.

Back off, she warned telepathically. *You want him to rage out again in the middle of class?*

Jason met her gaze, but only smiled. A second later he turned that smile to Alexander.

"You have a protector."

The shifter followed his gaze with a furious scowl.

It seemed that at some point while he was bleeding out in the forest, Jason had discovered *exactly* how to get under the guy's skin. Why he would want to was another question entirely. But with the skill of a puppet-master, he leaned back to appreciate his work.

"Back off," Alexander fumed, unintentionally mimicking Aria's exact words right back to her. "I don't need your help."

Jason shrugged casually. "I think you probably do."

Aria forgot the shifter entirely and gave him a cold glare. "I think you're going to find yourself back in the infirmary if you aren't careful."

He flashed a charming smile then leaned back in his chair, fixing the shifter calmly in his sights. "I only meant it wouldn't be hard to imagine."

"What—"

"You killing someone in the middle of the night."

Alexander went perfectly rigid, like he'd received an electric shock. His eyes darted nervously to the people sitting closest before returning to Jason with a look that was hard to describe.

"What are you saying?" he asked quietly.

Yeah, what ARE you saying?

"I'm saying that I *did* think you might have something to do with Dorf," Jason replied evenly, never breaking the man's gaze. "...but I don't think that anymore."

If it was possible, Alexander looked even more surprised. He gripped the sides of the desk, almost like he was battling a physical state of whiplash, before shaking his head.

"Why not?"

Jason glanced up distractedly, as if he'd forgotten they were even talking. "He was killed quickly, wasn't he? A simple snap of the neck." His blue eyes locked on Alexander's dark ones before drifting once more around the room. "I don't think that's your style."

That was the last time either boy spoke for the rest of the period.

Grumbling under her breath about the dramatic tendencies of men, Aria proceeded to work on the project by herself—picking a random question about the construction of the school and sketching out a vague outline of the research it would entail. Her nerves were jumping and her mind was racing with other things, but unfortunately she had nothing but time.

After about forty minutes, she could stretch it out no further and dropped the pencil on the desk. Throwing bored glances around the room while silently lamenting her own misfortune.

Having grown up together, most of the Guilder student dynamics had been long since written in stone. When they were divided into pairs, you already knew who everyone would be choosing. But the addition of the three shifters had made for more than one interesting match.

Leona Wross, a shy girl with the power to bend sound waves, had been too slow on the draw and found herself sitting across from Eric Lach. From the looks of things, he was no more talkative one-on-one than he was in a group. They'd finished the assignment quickly and were sitting in perfect silence, both trying their best to ignore the other.

With an entire class of witnesses seated safely between them, Aria studied him closely—eyes sweeping over the sturdy legs. The rippling muscles. Now that she knew his secret, it wasn't at all difficult to imagine him as a lumbering bear. She wondered why she hadn't guessed it before.

Leona caught her staring and rolled her eyes, jerking her heads towards him as if to say, "Can you believe my luck getting stuck with this guy?" Aria flashed a sympathetic smile, cocking her head towards a problematic shifter of her own.

That being said, not everyone was having such a miserable time.

The sound of quiet laughter filtered through the air, and she turned to see Benji and Sofia sitting much closer than was required. Their heads were bent together, their arms were lightly touching, and their legs were crossed ever so casually beneath the desk. Every now and then, one would lean into the other as they whispered conspiratorially and laughed at some nonsense joke.

Typical Benji.

Best way to win his affection? Just attack him in the dead of night.

Alexander perked up when they laughed again, features sharpening like a dog on the hunt. A strange sort of growl rumbled in the back of his throat, but if Sofia heard it she certainly didn't pay any attention. She'd turned every bit of focus to the boy sitting across from her, the one with the easy smile and the sparkling blue eyes.

"Okay—two minutes! You should all be finishing up!"

Aria let out a sigh of relief as the students started gathering up their things. *Thank the Maker.*

"What did you pick?" Jason asked, glancing over the paper. His brow creased with a frown as he scanned down the side. "Construction?"

"Yeah. Construction." She swung her messenger bag angrily between them, making sure to hit his recently healed chest. "It seemed the safest bet, under the circumstances."

His gaze rested on her before he ripped a blank paper from his notebook and started scrawling hastily along the front. "Nah, let's do the security question instead."

Aria watched in astonishment as he framed it quickly as a thesis statement, adding all their names. Even Alexander paused beside his desk, glancing down in surprise.

"Really?" he asked dryly. "You want to investigate the murder?"

Jason's lips curved with the hint of a smile as his hand flew across the page. "Why not?"

The shifter clenched his jaw, trying to rein in his temper. "I don't know, maybe because the three of us are the prime suspects?"

Jason finished quickly and slipped the notebook into his bag.

"We were cleared," he said simply, eyes lingering on Alexander just a second too long. "We were all cleared of everything."

With that, he swept down the center of the room without a backwards glance—placing the paper on Dorian's desk before vanishing outside. Benji was still lingering with Sofia, purposely taking his time, but Aria and Alexander stared after him with matching looks of shock.

...post-traumatic insanity? Is that a thing?

She saw Dorian glance down at the paper, murmuring distracted farewells to the students passing by. His lips parted as they swept over the question, but by the time he lifted his eyes Jason was already gone.

...and so was Alexander.

Aria whirled around with a gasp, astonished that anyone could move so quickly. She hurried after him, sensing trouble, elbowing people out of her way.

He wasn't in the corridor. Neither was Jason.

He wasn't on the next floor. Neither was Jason.

Then she spotted them both on the lawn.

"Hey!"

She burst outside just as Alexander flew up behind him, grabbing him roughly by the coat. A group of freshmen stopped to watch but she waved them furiously onward, racing forward herself.

"What the hell is going on!" Alexander demanded, spinning him around so they were standing face to face. "First, you don't tell anyone what happened. And now—"

Jason yanked himself free, staring back with perfect calm. "Did you *want* me to tell them?"

Alexander's mouth opened, but he couldn't bring himself to say anything. He just stood there, glaring and trembling at the same time.

Jason held his gaze a moment, then shook his head. "Then why do you care?"

Aria reached them a second later, sliding to a stop between the two. Benji and Sofia had seen the confrontation from the class window and were paused by the door. Eric was just a step behind.

Alexander's hands balled into fists as he snarled between his teeth, "I don't owe you anything."

A flash of amusement brightened Jason's eyes. "Sure."

Another stalemate. Another impasse.

But this time there would be no retreat.

Alexander leaned even closer, just inches away from his face.

"You want to know how to murder someone on this campus?" he taunted. "You want to know how *I'd* do it? Meet me by the supply shed after midnight and we'll find out together."

Jason cocked his head with a chilling smile. "It's a date."

"THIS IS ALL YOUR FAULT!" Aria snapped, throwing a handful of sparks.

Benji jerked back on the bed, personally offended whenever his own power was used against him. "How the hell is it my fault? I'm not the one who spent an entire class taunting the guy."

Her eyes narrowed as little spirals of smoke drifted from her hands. "You know *exactly* what I'm talking about."

"Leave Benji alone," Jason ordered gently. "He didn't do anything."

Unlike the others, who'd been on high alert since hearing the words 'murder on campus', he was strangely relaxed. Throwing crumpled bits of paper into the bin with deadly accuracy.

"He *did*," Aria insisted, "but that's not the point. It's *you* I should be yelling at!"

He lifted his eyebrows with a look of adorable innocence.

"I don't see why there has to be yelling at all."

At that point, sparks started flying from Benji's hands as well. He abandoned his defensive position on the bed and came to stand at Aria's side. Together, they towered over him.

"Let me get this straight," he demanded. "First you turn us all into pariahs by insisting we pretend not to know the guy tried to maul you to death. Then you decide to let him kill you anyway by volunteering to go on a murder mystery adventure in the middle of the woods."

Jason's smile faltered with a hint of annoyance. "What makes you think he could kill me?"

There was a beat of silence.

"I had the privilege of being there the last time."

"That's enough!" Aria shouted. "There will be no killing, because there will be no murder mystery adventure to begin with. You're not going. That's final."

Jason turned from one to the other, all with that unshakable calm. "Is that right?"

Benji shocked him just on principle, while Aria kicked out the base of his chair.

"Stop doing that!" she demanded. "You know I hate it!"

"What?" he panted, picking himself up off the floor. When Benji aimed for him again, he countered with a trio of icicles that pinned the cheetah's sleeve to the wall. "You hate what?"

She rolled her eyes and paced across the room, melting the ice with a wave of her hand. "Your dad's weird calm thing. It doesn't work on you—you didn't grow up below ground."

Jason smirked, knowing very well it *did* work. "I wasn't aware that was a prerequisite."

She turned around slowly. "Don't make me set you on fire..."

The three friends had decided to ditch the rest of the afternoon classes, after the first turned out to be a disaster. Instead, they'd relocated to the boys' shared dorm and proceeded to tear into each other for the next hour and a half. Granted, she and Benji were the only ones doing the tearing. Jason had made himself some microwave popcorn and settled at his desk to watch.

"What do you think Lily's going to say about this?" Benji asked innocently.

Aria turned in triumph as the smirk melted off Jason's face.

The friends gave each other a lot of latitude, and their indulgence knew no end, but Lily Decker had a special place in his heart. Disappointing her was a kind of pain he'd rather avoid.

"Lily will understand..." he muttered.

The door swung open and a petite girl stood in the frame.

"What will I understand?"

Jason's lips parted before he shot a look of betrayal at the others.

It wasn't the first time they'd set him up in such a way. As the only two shifters in the group, they used their heightened sensitivity shamelessly to their own advantage.

"I, uh...I decided to make peace with Alexander," he began diplomatically. "No more fighting, Lilybell. Isn't that nice?"

She folded her arms slowly, dark eyes narrowing with suspicion. "It might be."

"It's even better than that," Benji added with a wicked grin. "They're *dating* now."

Another beat of silence.

Jason turned to him with a strained look.

"Why must you always be so helpful?"

"Hang on." Lily help up her hands, stepping in between them. "Somebody tell me what's going on right now. I hadn't even gotten through my math class before one of the shifters started yelling that Alexander Hastings and Jason Alden were about to have a fight on the front lawn."

Three people opened their mouths to answer, but she only had eyes for one.

"But you see, *that* didn't make any sense," she continued in a dangerous voice. "Because I told Jason that I was going to meet him right there in the hall—remember that, Jase?"

He drummed nervously on the side of his leg, looking for allies but finding none.

"Alexander invited him to come out tonight," Aria interjected, keeping her piercing gaze locked on him the entire time. "Apparently, they're going to discuss how to commit the perfect murder on campus. Or rather, Alexander volunteered to show him."

Lily stared a moment in shock, then rotated slowly to Jason.

"*...are you flippin' crazy?!*"

He sank onto the bed, rubbing his temples. "It certainly looks like it."

Another bolt of lightning was aimed and prepped, but she quickly stepped in between.

"I'm serious, Jase—what are you thinking?" Her eyes widened and her lovely face went pale. "Unless...unless you want to get him alone."

Aria looked at him with a surge of panic—she hadn't even considered *that* possibility.

"This has nothing to do with that," Jason said calmly. "If he's going to be staying here, then he's going to be staying here. We might as well make the most of it. And if that means having a midnight showdown to bury the hatchet, that's exactly what I intend to do."

"But why?" Benji insisted. "Why are you interested in burying the hatchet at all?" He shook his head disapprovingly. "You have to admit, it's not exactly our style."

Jason flashed a tired grin. "Yeah, but a showdown is."

Lily shook her head briskly, straightening her coat. "We'll just have to make sure it's one he'll never forget."

The others nodded slowly, but Jason leapt to his feet in alarm.

"Wait—no! You guys aren't coming. He and I are supposed to go alone."

Benji rolled his eyes, as if it was never even a question, while Aria leapt on the bandwagon with a sarcastic glare. If his mind wasn't to be changed, they'd just have to join them.

"Of course we're coming," she snapped. "You can bet his friends will be there."

"They won't," Jason argued, with a certainty that couldn't possibly be real. "They wouldn't."

"And how do you know?"

"Because that's not the way these things are done!"

"I could just ask Sofia..." Benji said tentatively, pulling out his phone.

Aria stared in shock for a moment before thundering at the top of her lungs. "You got her number?!"

The walls shook as the shouting continued anew. Lightning flashed back and forth, and the students watching from the lawn shook their heads with the same knowing smile.

The Kerrigan kids might not have openly invited scandal.

But it sure seemed to follow wherever they went...

Chapter 8

That night, the trouble started before it could even begin.

Aria crept down the first flight of stairs without a problem, meeting Lily in her room. The plan had been to sneak outside together. One would scan ahead with advanced senses for faculty prowling the premises, while the other would keep an eye on their retreat—simultaneously trying to access the future at the same time. Thus far, tapping into her newfound clairvoyance had been a problem. But between the murder and the fight, it wasn't like she'd had a lot of time to try.

The second she reached the door Aria turned invisible, then pressed her mouth to the frame—cooing twice in her best impersonation of a dove. Lily's roommate opened the door with a sarcastic grin.

"Considering who your parents are, you guys should really get a better signal."

Aria melted back into sight with a cool glare, glancing inside to where Lily was lacing up her boots in the corner. "Considering who my parents are, you should really shut up."

She slipped inside a moment later, closing the door behind her as her gaze drifted impatiently around the room. It was just as fantastical as her own—only a good deal cleaner. Thanks to Lily's rather indulgent parents, both she and her roommate Hallie boasted in-floor heating, an impressive library, and a half-hidden jacuzzi. Her coat was hanging beside a Rembrandt on the wall.

"You're late," she chided. "We were supposed to meet at eleven-fifty. And it's—"

"—exactly eleven-fifty?" Lily finished zipping up her coat, then swept out her long ivory hair. Unlike the rest of the girls living in Aumbry Hall, she was able to look upon the famous Aria Wardell without a hint of fear. "Yeah, I saw that too."

Hallie dropped her eyes with a smile, while Aria pretended not to hear.

"Anyway, we should get going."

Lily nodded and slipped a few seemingly innocuous things into her pocket. A tube of lipstick that didn't match the color she was wearing, a paperclip, a nail file...

Aria frowned when she saw the file. "You planning on giving yourself a little manicure tonight?"

The girl shrugged innocently. "You never know."

Aria hesitated in the doorway, eyeing the jacket warily. "You know, I read that interrogation report of your mom's, too—"

"We should get going. Don't want to be late."

Hallie waved them off, settling in for a night of movies and popcorn. After so many years, she was well-used to her roommate's eccentric friends and late-night adventures. If the need for an alibi ever arose, she was usually Lily's first call.

The girls were already down the first flight of stairs by the time Aria sat down. In escapes like this, speed was key. There might not have been any sign of Madame Elpis so far, but the woman was as much a part of the women's dormitory as the ancient stone. Shortly after she died, they could be sure to find her haunting the place. It was only a matter of time before she saw them now.

"This is *ridiculously* unfair," Lily hissed, sliding to a stop at the base of the third floor. "Until you can make all of us invisible, I don't think you should be allowed to use it for yourself."

Aria flashed a grin she would never see. "Feeling nervous?"

The psychic smacked blindly at her shoulder and happened to make contact. "Feeling like, when this woman rounds the corner, I'll be the only one getting expelled."

Aria rematerialized beside her, slipping into the fennec fox tatù. There wasn't a whisper of sound on the stairwell, but both girls knew how quickly that could change.

"Maybe if you could manage a vision, we could avoid things like that."

Lily shot her a glare. "Oh—like you were so great the second you got ink."

"I was magnificent." Aria tilted back her head with a nostalgic smile; her father's fox tatù had been the first she'd been able to mimic. "Tales will be written of my greatness."

Lily shot her a look.

"I remember you falling down a lot."

They continued racing down the stairs without another word—startling at every noise and peering anxiously around the corners. They were supposed to meet the boys on the lawn at exactly midnight, but the boys wouldn't have this kind of problem. The man in charge of Joist Hall was about five hundred years old, and split his time between naps and pinochle. After Benji and Jason bribed him with a bottle of Scotch their freshman year, they virtually had the run of the place.

"Just a little bit farther," Aria panted, glancing out the window to see a pair of dark figures already moving across the lawn. "Once we get to the landing, we can just jump—"

A sudden creak echoed up the stairwell.

Both girls froze, holding their breath and listening. At any moment they expected to see the frigid housemistress sweeping up the stairs, but nothing happened. After a few drawn-out seconds, they relaxed their position and let out a simultaneous breath.

"Just the wind," Aria murmured. "Come on, let's get moving."

They picked up the pace, rounded the curve, then let out a silent scream as they nearly collided with someone racing up in the opposite direction. There was a frantic tangle of legs and arms before the three girls were able to separate themselves.

"Sofia?" Aria gasped, pulling herself straight.

The girl looked just as surprised as they were—with saucer-like eyes, pale skin, and a jacket thrown haphazardly over one arm. She opened her mouth, then threw a glance over her shoulder.

"That woman who oversees the dormitory? Madame...something?"

"Elpis," Aria and Lily answered in unison.

"She's coming!"

Together, the three girls spun on their heels and headed straight back up the way they'd come—leaping the stairs three at a time, mentally calculating how long it would take a woman five times their age to complete the same journey. They'd just made it to the landing between the fourth and fifth floor, when Aria grabbed both girls by the wrist and yanked them into the bathroom.

"Won't she check in here?" Sofia panted. Shifters had a natural endurance, but the sight of the woman rampaging around in curlers was enough to steal anyone's breath.

"I expect she will," Aria said calmly. "But we won't be here to see it."

The girl shook her head in confusion but Lily was already moving to the far window, unhinging the ancient lock. It sprang free and a rush of freezing air poured into the bathroom.

A second after that, the idea suddenly clicked.

"Oh, no—you guys can't be serious!"

Lily swung a leg out the window, while Aria flashed a faint grin.

"It's not as bad as it looks. We've done it loads of times before."

"I only broke my leg once," Lily added helpfully, her voice echoing from somewhere outside. "But to be fair, I was attacked halfway down by a rogue pigeon..."

Sofia blanched, unable to process anything more than the window.

"We're so high up," she whispered, casting a terrified glance back at the door. "Is there anything to even hold on to—"

"Don't come," Aria said simply. The two might have bonded under a temporary truce the night before, but they were still on opposite sides. "I don't know why you're out of bed anyway."

Sofia's eyes narrowed sarcastically. "For exactly the same reason you are. To make sure those boys don't kill each other."

"Arie?" Lily's voice drifted inside. "Can you check for birds?"

Aria distractedly moved toward the window, glancing down at the drop. "I highly doubt that's the only reason."

Sofia flushed. "What's that supposed to mean?"

The girls locked eyes, both picturing the same red-haired man. A moment later Aria returned to the window, swinging her leg over the ledge.

"It means if you want to come—this is the only way to do it."

She vanished a moment later, half-hoping the girl wouldn't follow. By this point, though, she should have known better. There was a quiet sigh then Sofia appeared above her, staring down at the lawn.

"This is...*really* high."

At one point or another, each of the friends had said the same thing. But after years of becoming inured to such antics, the fear had given way to adrenaline and glee.

"Try not to think about it," Aria advised, already halfway down herself. "Think of the trouble waiting if you stay—it's great motivation."

Unseen by anyone else Sofia rolled her eyes, at the same time digging her nails into the slick stone. "You should be a life-coach, you know that?"

"Twenty-four seconds," Lily whispered triumphantly, throwing up her hands the second she touched down. "A personal best in terms of time."

"Nothing compared to *my* time," Aria boasted, dropping down beside her. "But we can't all be gifted with such glorious ink."

Lily smacked her with a grin and the two of them started heading towards the trees. A second later, they remembered Sofia and glanced back at the wall.

"She'll be fine," Aria muttered. "Let's just go."

Lily gave her a long look. "Fine, fine...I was just kidding."

They jogged briskly back to the tower, getting there just as the lovely girl released her death grip on the stone and fell lightly to their side.

"I did it!" she exclaimed, unable to hide her excitement. She tilted her head back with a grin, peering all the way back to the top. "I can't believe that just happened!"

Unfortunately for the others, she had one of those contagious smiles—and they soon found themselves grinning as well. Of course they stopped it quickly, scowling instead.

"You want to take a picture?" Aria challenged. "Or can we go?"

The shifter's smile faded slightly as Lily spun around with a dainty sniff. "Seriously, Hastings. A child could make that climb."

Not another word was said between them as the three girls darted across the lawn, safe under the cover of the trees. It only took a second before two people started walking towards them.

Granted, it wasn't the two people Aria expected to see.

"What are you doing here?" Alexander demanded, looking just as surprised to see them as they were surprised themselves. "It's bad enough I'm stuck with..."

Eric folded his bulging arms, daring him to finish the sentence.

"You didn't really think I'd let you go alone, did you?" Sofia asked briskly, sweeping her long hair up into a ponytail. "Someone has to temper the insanity."

"Yeah, because you're so stable yourself," he retorted, but he didn't look particularly angry. In fact, Aria could have sworn she saw the hint of a smile. That smile brightened significantly when his gaze fell on her. "What about you, Wardell? Keeping tabs on me?"

Her teeth ground together and she reminded herself they were there to make peace. "You're not the person I'm here to see."

Even as she spoke there was a rustling in the trees, and two new people stepped out of the shadows. They stopped abruptly when they saw the group waiting for them, stilling in surprise.

"Looks like the gang's all here," Benji said brightly, shooting Sofia a secret grin. He lowered his voice slightly and added to Jason, "Told you he'd bring someone."

For his part, Jason didn't look at all pleased. That being said, he hadn't expected his friends to sit on the sidelines while he volunteered to wander into the darkness with a man who'd recently attempted to take his life. He glanced at them briefly, then bowed his head with a frustrated sigh.

Alexander missed nothing, stepping forward with his hands in the air.

"All right, let's just get it all out in the open. Yes—I may have gotten a little rough with your friend the other night. And yes—he covered for me. Though I have no bloody idea why." He glanced briefly at Jason before turning back to the others. "The point is, it's not going to happen again, all right? Scout's honor. So there's no need for the chaperones."

Only then did Aria realize that Eric's grip on Alexander was just as tight as Benji's was on Jason. Though whether it was to restrain or protect wasn't quite clear.

Once the little speech was finished, the shifter glanced about to see how it had gone over.

...not well.

"So that's it?" Lily took a step into the space between them. She may have been the youngest person there, the only one who hadn't yet learned to tap into her powers, but she stepped forward without a hint of fear. Standing head-to-head with the tiger. "Forgive and forget? You could have *killed* him, Hastings. If Aria hadn't done her healing..." She shook her head. "You think this is settled with a 'Trust me, it won't happen again'?"

Alexander stared down at her, then lifted his shoulder with a shrug. "His rules. Not mine."

"Not mine either," Lily answered in a low voice, clutching those secret items she'd stashed in her pocket. "But this *will* be settled. One day. I can promise you that."

A chill swept over the clearing. The lovely girl had so much in common with her father it was sometimes easy to forget that she was Angela Cross' daughter, down to the bone.

Alexander froze in spite of himself, then forced a smile. "Until that day, sweetheart."

Yeah, until that day.

"Shall we move this along?" Aria said quickly, before things could spiral into an unfortunate sequel. "What exactly were the two of you planning on doing tonight?"

Jason turned to Alexander, interested to hear the answer himself.

"Isn't it obvious?" The shifter spread his arms wide, gesturing to the campus. "One of your teachers was murdered on-site. We're going to figure out how that happened."

The others stiffened with the same distasteful look. Even when the things he was saying were technically correct, his callous tone was enough to set their teeth on edge.

Benji clenched his jaw, trying to keep his temper in check. "Let me guess—out of the goodness of your heart?"

The shifter's eyes danced with amusement. "Don't be silly. It happens to be my research question."

AFTER THE PRELIMINARY threats had been made and everyone present was fairly convinced they weren't going to be suddenly massacred by the other side, the unlikely consortium set out through the trees towards the perimeter. While only some parts of the campus had been cordoned off by a fence, the invisible boundary was silently understood by everyone who crossed it. Like dogs trained with a shock collar, they instinctively stepped back once they'd gotten too close.

"Well it certainly doesn't look like much," Alexander murmured, kneeling down to examine the space for himself. The air shimmered slightly and he retracted his hand. "Or maybe not."

"I wouldn't," Benji advised, staying well clear himself. "You never know what's going to happen; if it will shock you, freeze you, or just trigger a silent alarm to call in the—"

"Agents," Jason hissed, swiftly pulling him behind a tree.

The rest of them melted quickly into the shadows as a trio of men rounded the curve of a building just twenty feet away. Under most circumstances they would have been sitting ducks, but these men weren't looking for anything in particular. If anything, it looked like they were simply on a break. They were standing behind the Oratory in clothes typically used for training, laughing quietly amongst themselves and sipping from bottles of purified water. Not an immediate threat, but the fact remained...they certainly *would* have been to anyone who'd tried to break in to the school.

"This whole part of the campus is out," Jason murmured under his breath, slipping into the trees with the others. "No one in their right mind would try breaking in this close to the Oratory."

"The northern wing is out, too," Lily added. "It's too close to Tristan's office."

The others started nodding in agreement, but one person was shaking her head.

"That's assuming whoever it was knew where Tristan's office is," Sofia argued. "It's also assuming Dorf was even the target—which seems unlikely."

Aria lifted her eyebrows in surprise. The lovely shifter usually kept her opinions to herself, especially in the presence of her overbearing brother. But this one didn't make any sense.

"What do you mean, not the target?" she repeated with a frown. "His neck got snapped."

"It was dark," Eric said gruffly. "It was quick."

Aria's surprise tripled on the spot.

He can talk?

"The man had no enemies, no grudges held against him," Sofia continued softly. "He lived quietly on campus with very little social life outside the school. If we're serious about looking into all the possibilities, we have to consider the man was simply in the wrong place at the wrong time."

A silence fell over the clearing.

Aria and her friends thought they'd been so clever, taking matters into their own hands. But it was clear now, they weren't the only ones who'd been investigating the murder.

It was quiet for a moment, then Jason broke the silence.

"How do you know all that?"

Sofia's eyes flashed with sarcasm, then cooled immediately when they drifted down to the newly healed skin on his chest. "They might have brought in you, Oliver, and Aria that night, but let's be clear—my brother was the prime suspect. You think I'm not going to take an interest? You think I'm not going to do everything I can to clear him?"

"And what if he's guilty?" Lily replied coldly. "We all know he's capable."

The shifter's eyes flashed again, but the psychic was merely protective—just as protective as she was herself. "Your own aunt cleared him."

If only that was enough for the Council.

"Maybe you want to start talking *to* me instead of just *about* me," Alexander said loudly.

Lily shot a dangerous look in his direction, but it was Sofia who spun on her heel.

"Shut up."

A gasp of surprise rippled through the clearing. Even the stoic Eric looked shaken to the core. Alexander took a second to regain his composure, then began, "I only meant—"

"I could give a *damn* what you meant," his sister interrupted, looking two seconds away from showing him what a tiger attack felt like from the other side. "Do you think she's wrong to be angry? Do you think they're wrong to suspect you?" A pale finger flew into the air, pointing blindly at Jason's chest. "You almost *killed* the guy, you stupid moron! Over a stupid high school dance! So yeah, I think you can take whatever criticism they choose to throw at you and *shut the hell up!*"

A silent shockwave went through the trees.

Alexander was stunned. Benji was in love. But Aria was thoughtful—ignoring the threats and latching on to something she'd said earlier, about their talk with Natasha.

"My aunt doesn't see everything," she murmured, almost to herself. Her eyes drifted to her friends, uncertain whether to share the secret. "There are things she can miss."

Alexander's eyes flickered up with a knowing glimmer. She flushed and looked away.

Not that.

The group response was hardly definitive. Lily was looking hesitant, Benji was looking at Sofia, and Jason's face had flushed scarlet at the memory of their stolen kiss.

After a few drawn-out seconds, she decided to take matters into her own hands.

"There was a shadow," she blurted suddenly, before she could lose the nerve. "The night of the murder. I couldn't tell who it was, but it was streaking away from the history building. *Fast.*"

This one little bit of news stopped the conversation.

"A shadow?" Eric repeated with a brutish frown. "That's what you're going on? A shadow?"

On second thought, maybe it's better if he doesn't speak at all.

"A person or a shifter?" Alexander asked sharply.

Aria shook her head. "A person, I think. But it was too quick for me to tell. Since then we've been...we've been looking through the tatù registry for anyone with that kind of ink."

Three shifters exchanged a glance.

"How do you have access to the registry?"

Benji was quick to shut the question down. "It doesn't matter. The point is, there's way too many people that qualify to narrow down the list."

The group paused again, thinking.

"Then where was it headed?" Alexander asked suddenly.

Aria lifted her head. "What?"

"This...shadow. Which direction was it headed?"

She glanced instinctively at Benji, then shook her head. "*Away* from the murder. They were fleeing the scene. What does it matter which way?"

Alexander opened his mouth to speak, then glanced at Jason and seemed to think better of it. After a few seconds of silent deliberation, he chose his next words very carefully.

"Exactly—he was fleeing the scene." His skin flushed ever so slightly as he fidgeted uneasily under their gaze. "I've recently come to understand that in moments like that, you don't think about covering your tracks—you get to where you need to go. It's your best chance of escape."

The friends glanced at each other before turning back to the school.

From where they were standing, they could see the corner of the history building peeking out from the western wing. Aria lifted her finger, tracing the path the shadow took.

Sure enough, it was a straight line—heading straight for a cottage.

"Who lives there?" Sofia asked, following her gaze.

Lily shook her head, forgetting for a moment that she'd decided to hate the girl until the end of time. "Don't know—the vacancies shift depending on who's teaching that semester and which agents are in from out of town." She cocked her head thoughtfully. "There's not much security."

"Why would they need security?" Sofia mumbled. "The people living there *are* security all to themselves."

It was a fair point. There were houses it was safe to break in to, and houses it wasn't. The last thing you'd want was to break one of these windows or knock down one of these doors. There was simply no way of knowing what kind of firepower was waiting on the other side.

Then again, the cottage in question was set slightly away from the rest—on the far edge of the lawn beside the tree-line. If there was ever a chance to see who lived inside, this was it.

"I'll go," Aria murmured, turning invisible at the same time. For this kind of recon, she was the natural choice. Her eyes flickered to Benji. "Cover me?"

He nodded even without seeing her, knowing instinctively the question was for him. The others waved them on impatiently, well-used to such things, but the three shifters were watching in open fascination. Eric, with all the tact of a cave troll, waved his arm blindly, trying to find her.

"Not feeling so cocky now are you, bear?"

Alexander rolled his eyes and swatted his arm out of the air.

After taking a deep breath, Aria crouched down low and darted towards the cottage. Her chosen ink might have rendered her invisible, but old habits were hard to break. She flew from tree to tree, using their cover as long as she could before sprinting across the open grass.

As usual, Benji was right by her side. He might not have had supernatural shielding like she did, but his tatù made him fast enough that no one looking would be able to see.

The windows were dark, but uncovered. Smoke was rising from the chimney, but there wasn't a sound from inside. After mentally debating whether to switch to a silent tatù, Aria decided to stick with invisibility and began climbing silently up the flowering hedge.

"You got this," Benji breathed, keeping his eyes on her progress by watching the denting of the leaves beneath her hands. "I'm right below you."

If anyone else had said such a thing, she would have scoffed and shut them down. But it was always comforting coming from Benji. The two might compete for having the biggest ego in the group, but those things never seemed to matter when they were only around each other.

One hand in front of the other.

It was the same thing she told herself every time she climbed the trellis beneath her bedroom window. Of course, it was much easier going down than it was going up.

"Any time, Wardell," Benji murmured, standing like a guard beneath her.

She gritted her teeth, wishing desperately she'd decided to go with a strength tatù after all. "You want to try?"

"Absolutely," he replied instantly, putting his hands on the base of the ivy.

But Jason appeared from nowhere, pulling him back.

"Be quiet," he commanded under his breath. "She's almost there."

After a few more agonizing seconds, her fingers finally curled over the ledge. By now all the others were gathered beneath her, but she never saw them. She was staring intently through the window, trying to make out anything she could in the dark.

Then suddenly, another face appeared on the other side.

Crap!

She let out a silent gasp, almost losing her grip entirely, then remembered she was invisible and held her position. There was a suspended moment where he stared right through her.

Then the man vanished and she dropped back to the ground.

"What happened?" Benji caught her instinctively, setting her on the grass as she shimmered back into sight. "Who was it?"

She lifted her eyes slowly to the window.

"...it was Dorian Locke."

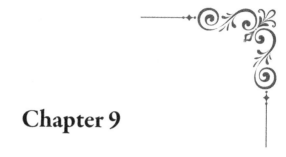

Chapter 9

The midnight hour came and passed, and still the group stood there debating it—hidden deep within the trees. As fate would have it, they weren't far from where the attack had happened the night of the dance. Jason's eyes kept glazing over. He shivered involuntarily, zipping up his coat.

"Why would it be Dorian?" Lily asked, shaking her head. "It doesn't make any sense."

"He's the newest one here," Benji murmured. "No connections, no grievances. Most of the parents haven't met him yet. I doubt people outside the university circle even know he works at the school."

"Wait a second," Alexander interrupted. "Are you saying *he* was the real target?"

"He was a history teacher at his last job," Jason remembered quietly. "Maybe someone heard he was working here and decided to come looking. Started in the history building."

Benji's eyes flickered up to the building in question. Aria knew what he was thinking. His father taught history at Guilder as well. It could easily have been him.

No, it couldn't, she corrected herself.

Luke might not have had a tatù, but the man could hold his own against anything the supernatural world tried to throw at him. There was a reason he was included in the deadly Kerrigan gang. No one in their right mind would try coming after him; they wouldn't survive it.

Dorf was a different story.

The man was gentle, trusting. His ink wasn't dangerous. She remembered the story Dorian told her at the library—how he'd helped with luggage, given the librarian an impromptu tour. He'd encouraged her to apologize for her outburst, reminding her the teacher was a good man.

Maybe Sofia was right. Maybe he was just in the wrong place at the wrong time.

"Why wasn't Dorian killed, then?" Eric asked impatiently, gesturing to the cottage. "You say this killer shadow ran straight here—probably after realizing his mistake. So why is he alive?"

"Because he wasn't at the cottage," Aria said immediately. "He was supervising my detention in the library. Remember he wasn't promoted to the teaching staff until afterwards."

Benji nodded slowly, eyes flickering between the cottage and the school. "Well, if Dorian actually *was* the real target, then the killer's job isn't done. If they risked it once, they'll risk it again. My guess is they'll be back as soon as the heat has died down."

Alexander followed his gaze before throwing Jason an unexpected grin. "At least some good came of our little skirmish in the woods..."

The rest of them turned to him in shock. Even Jason, who'd kept such a level head so far, found himself at a temporary loss for words. "...excuse me?"

Alexander froze, then glanced quickly at his sister. "I just meant—agents were sent out to patrol afterwards. If the killer really is waiting for an opening, at least our fight set him back a few days."

"So you make a bloody joke about it?" Sofia hissed under her breath.

"What?" Alexander threw up his hands. "I was *trying* to be friendly."

Strangely enough, Aria believed he was telling the truth. She held up her hand, silencing the sibling quarrel before it could even begin.

There was only room for one brother-sister blood feud in the group, and she and James had claimed it years before.

"It physically pains me to say it, but Alexander's right. There *are* agents on patrol." She stared warily into the darkness. "The problem is, they're patrolling for the wrong guy."

"In that case, we'll just have to patrol ourselves," Benji said briskly. "Keep an eye on things around *this* part of campus, at least until we can confirm it's Dorian."

Sofia nodded excitedly, pleased they were finally making progress. "We can break into shifts," she suggested. "Set up a surveillance—"

"No...*we* won't," Lily interrupted, bringing the conversation to a sudden halt. Her dark eyes flickered between the two groups, lingering on Alexander. "I don't know what kind of power-play was supposed to happen tonight, but you've clearly done enough. We'll take it from here."

In a flash, that collective spirit they'd been building for the last hour vanished in the cold night air. Aria and Jason nodded soundly in agreement. Benji avoided Sofia's eyes.

The girl stared at them, trying not to look as hurt as she felt.

"We're in this together," she began uncertainly. "They're accusing my brother—"

"Yeah?" Lily snapped. "At least someone is."

Jason flinched beside her, then turned away.

However divisive it might be, the psychic was right. No matter how the night had been originally intended, it had served its purpose. The truce was over now. Never to be restored.

But Sofia wasn't going down without a fight.

"Look," she started as she took a step forward, speaking with strained patience, "I understand that you're angry. I'd be furious myself. But this isn't—"

RUN!

The message rang out telepathically between them, but it had come too late. The friends had been bickering so heatedly, even the shifters hadn't heard the agent coming. By the time he stepped into the clearing, the game was over. There was nowhere to run, nowhere to hide.

...or so they thought.

The moment played out like it was in slow motion. There was a flash of surprise when the agent saw them, followed by a flash of recognition when he identified the kids. He was still stepping towards them when Lily threw up her hands—an involuntary reaction of half-surrender, half-surprise.

Then the strangest thing happened...the man froze.

"We're sorry!" she shrieked, flushing in shame. "We'll just go back to the dorms—"

"Lily." Benji put a hand on her shoulder, staring at the man in surprise.

"We didn't realize it had gotten so late," the psychic trilled nervously, still addressing the frozen man. "We were just working on a class project and—"

"*Lily,*" Benji said again, taking a cautious step forward. "He's not moving."

"...what?"

All her panic stalled as she realized what had happened for the first time. A look of total bewilderment flashed across her face as she slowly looked down at her hands.

"I-I didn't..."

There was a charged moment where no one knew what to say. The first time a person accessed their ink was a momentous occasion—one they'd remember for the rest of their lives.

But it wasn't supposed to happen like this.

Of all people, it was Alexander who broke the silence. The second he realized the agent was truly immobile, he fearlessly strode forward—waving a hand in front of the guy's face.

"Cool."

"He can still see you," Benji hissed furiously, swatting down his hand. His eyes flickered to the agent a moment later, muttering under his breath. "...sorry."

"Arie—erase the memory."

Aria turned in shock, but Lily had never been more upset. She was literally standing on the tips of her toes, wringing her hands in a cartoonish portrait of guilt.

"Erase the memory of a PC agent?!" she exclaimed. "Are you crazy?!"

"This is an attack!" Lily shrieked back, unable to control her volume. When Jason put a hand on her shoulder, she batted it away. "This is technically an attack—I'm using my power on an agent of the Privy Council!" Her eyes welled up with tears as she turned to the man in question. "And I'm so sorry about that, Mr. Jeffreys. I don't know how to control it—"

"So you want me to erase his memory?" Aria hissed between gritted teeth. "Because *this* is an accident, Lily. But *that* is very much intentional."

Alexander chuckled under his breath, finding the entire situation highly amusing. "Allow me to repeat what was recently said to me...he can hear you."

"Just do it," Lily whispered, tears spilling down her cheeks. "Please, Arie. I can't..."

She didn't finish, but she didn't have to. There weren't many things the friends wouldn't do for each other. Least of all when it was Lily. Least of all when Lily was crying.

"Fine," Aria sighed, stepping forward, "but get your butts back to the dorms. It's hard enough doing this once. I'm not going to do it again when he asks why we're out after curfew."

The others didn't have to be told twice. The second her back was turned, they vanished into the trees. Flying across the lawn so fast, she could easily imagine any one of them had a speed tatù.

"I really am sorry about this, Mr. Jeffreys." She bit her lip with a flush. "If it makes you feel any better, we weren't technically doing anything wrong—besides the curfew thing."

While he couldn't technically move, she could have sworn he still managed to roll his eyes.

"At any rate, I swear we'll go to sleep right after this is done—"

But at that moment, Lily put too much distance between them and the freezing power suddenly lifted. The man lurched forward to complete his step, while Aria's hands flew into the air.

In an instant, his eyes drifted out of focus—staring at her with a strange sort of calm.

"Uh...hi." She waved her hand nervously, trying to come up with something to say. "So, I know you're out here on patrol, but the thing is, you didn't find anything. In fact, it got so boring that you decided to go into the Oratory to train."

When he continued to stare at her, she felt compelled to add a bit more.

"But you're going to have an *amazing* night. You'll take a bubble bath, listen to your favorite music. And if anyone asks, the last name in the world you're going to say is Aria Wardell."

He blinked slowly, then headed off into the trees.

Please say that worked.

She streaked off towards the dormitories a second later, unwilling to push her luck any farther. Her feet barely skimmed the dewy grass as she slipped into Benji's own cheetah tatù—moving so quickly she didn't see the others until he grabbed her hand.

"Whoa there," he chuckled, letting go before the bone could snap. "Take a breath."

She took several in quick succession, trying to control her pounding heart. Then she lifted her gaze to see the rest of them standing in a loose crescent in front of her, trying hard not to smile.

"What?" she asked in bewilderment, feeling her hair to check for leaves. "What's so funny?"

Jason and Lily exchanged a quick look between them before he stepped forward with a grin.

"Did you just tell that agent to take a bubble bath?"

Aria froze where she stood, remembering too late that several of the others were gifted with advanced hearing. At this point, it would do no good to deny it. But she was still going to try.

"...no."

A tittering of laughter swept over the moonlit stone. Even Alexander, whose smiles were few and far between, couldn't help joining in. Only Lily remained silent, owing her a great debt.

"Leave her alone," she commanded, trying hard to keep a straight face. "She just saved each and every one of us. Are you really going to criticize how?"

Benji nudged her with a grin. "Yeah, but she saved some of us more than others. Isn't that right, Decker?"

Lily's cheeks flushed a delicate shade of pink as she avoided his eyes. "...I don't know what you mean."

Unfortunately, that only made the others laugh harder. After a few minutes Aria couldn't help but join them, still trying to catch her breath as she pressed her hands onto her knees.

"Let's just get inside," she finally panted. "There have been too many close calls..."

She straightened up slowly, turning white as a sheet. The others took one look at her face then whirled around themselves, freezing dead still when they saw the man standing behind them.

"I think that's a good idea," Gabriel said softly. "You kids should get inside. Everyone except you." His gaze fell on Jason. "You're coming with me."

NEVER HAD ARIA SEEN a group of teenagers obey a command so quickly.

The shifters were gone before Gabriel had even finished speaking—flying off towards their separate dormitories like ghosts in the night. Benji and Lily lingered only a second longer, shooting quick looks at Jason and mumbling apologies to their uncle under their breath. When it became clear that nothing they did was going to help they vanished as well, slipping past the stone doors.

In the end, only Aria remained.

"Uncle Gabriel, we were just..." She trailed off, wanting to help but unable to find the words to do so. "This was just a stupid thing for school."

Gabriel lifted his head slowly, looking away from Jason for the first time. Their eyes met for a fleeting moment and she flushed in shame, head bowing to her chest automatically.

"I'll just...see you guys later."

She turned on her heel to go, feeling like a monster to leave one of their number behind. But at the last second, a voice rang out between them.

Stay.

Her body froze, but her heart was pounding. She knew that voice as well as her own, but there was a different cadence to it. A cadence that was new, but one she was already coming to recognize as having come from someone's mind instead of their mouth.

Her breathing hitched as she glanced back at Jason.

He hadn't said it out loud. He didn't know she could even hear it.

He simply desired it with all his heart.

"I'd like to stay."

Gabriel was impassive, but Jason looked up in surprise.

"It's fine, Arie. Just get back to the dorms—"

"I'm staying," she repeated, shooting a quick glance at her uncle. "If that's okay."

Gabriel didn't say a word. He simply stared at her with that same unreadable expression before turning suddenly and heading across the grass. Jason and Aria exchanged a quick look then hurried immediately after him, flitting along in his shadow without daring to speak.

It wasn't a long walk. The Aldens were staying in one of the cottages within sight of the dorms. And yet it still gave Aria plenty of time to think.

It was no wonder he'd heard them, she realized with a flush of shame. When evading her uncle, most people thought it best to put entire countries between them. He was staying at Guilder specifically to keep an eye on his son. Had they really thought they could run around playing midnight detective without him noticing what was going on?

Her eyes flitted to the boy walking beside her. Like his father, it was impossible to look at his face and tell much of what was going on. The guy was a vault—opening only to certain people and only at certain times. Then again, why guess when you could know for sure?

With a silent surge of concentration, Aria focused on the new set of ink buzzing beneath her skin. It rose obediently to the surface, just waiting for her command.

But nothing seemed to happen.

Come on...just work.

She tried again, but with no better luck. There weren't any clear, decipherable thoughts. But while he might not have been thinking clearly, he was feeling everything. The man's face was a war of emotions. Everything from apprehension to uncertainty, to downright fatigue. But there was one feeling that won out over all the rest. And, given their present circumstances, it surprised her.

...rage?

The second they were within sight of the cottage, Jason left the others behind and stormed on ahead—yanking the door open and slamming it shut behind him. A shiver ran over Aria's skin. Gabriel paused where he stood, eyes locked intently on the front of the cottage.

"I want to help him," he said softly. "But I don't understand what's going on."

Aria's shoulders sank miserably as she followed his gaze. This fight might have technically started on the night of the dance, but it went back farther than that. In fact, she was suddenly convinced it went all the way back to a dingy little apartment on the outskirts of London.

"He's not...he's not *trying* to make you angry," she said tentatively, unsure what else she could say. Of all the secrets she'd ever been told, this one certainly wasn't hers to tell.

Gabriel sighed, digging his hands into his pockets. "I know that."

They stood there in silence for a while, listening to Jason bang about inside the house. From the sounds of things, he was trying to make coffee. But with a lot of noise, and very little success.

"Aria, if he was ever in actual *trouble*...you would tell me."

It wasn't exactly phrased as a question, but it hung between them all the same. Aria turned her head in the darkness, struck to the core by the sadness on her uncle's face.

"Yes, I would." She slipped her hand into his. "I promise."

He glanced down at her, then gave her fingers a quick squeeze. "Let's get inside. Before they charge me for property damages."

BY THE TIME THEY STEPPED inside the cottage, the idea of coffee had been abandoned and Jason was sitting on the sofa by the fire. Surprisingly enough, he wasn't alone. A statuesque woman was sitting in the opposite arm chair, eyes flickering in the light of the flames.

"Aunt Angel!"

At first Aria was surprised to see her, then she wasn't at the same time. Gabriel might have been the one to adopt Jason, but Angel had always felt responsible for him as well. He'd come to think of her as a second mother. She'd come to treat him as a son.

Angel's eyes flickered up and she smiled faintly in welcome. But she'd been witness to the rage-fest in the kitchen, and was quietly bracing for whatever was to come.

As it turned out, she didn't have to wait long.

"I want you to tell me about my parents."

Gabriel froze in the doorway, still in the process of taking off his shoes. However he'd imagined this conversation going, that certainly wasn't the opening question.

There was a moment of silence, then he pulled up a chair.

"What would you like to know?"

Aria let out a silent sigh of relief.

That's exactly what she loved about her uncle. He may have just caught them sneaking around campus with the one person they were supposed to avoid. He may have been angry enough to rampage around the kitchen himself. But he was somehow able to see past all that. To set his own feelings aside and do whatever needed to be done in the moment to help his son.

"Everything."

The others were sitting, but Jason now stood in between them. Gaze jumping from person to person as he paced furiously in front of the fire.

"My father," he turned to look at Angel instead, "you knew him best?"

She nodded slowly, legs tucked into the chair. "I dated him off and on for years. We basically grew up together."

Jason stopped his pacing for a split second.

"Then what happened?" he snapped.

She glanced swiftly at Gabriel before returning her eyes to his son.

"I broke it off with him when Cromfield sent me after Julian."

Jason nodded quickly and the pacing began anew. Aria watched carefully, twisting her fingers in her lap. So far, none of this was new information. The gang had often teased that Angel could have easily been his mother instead. But they were on the brink of something, coming up fast.

"...and my mother?"

There it is.

Aria gripped the edge of her chair as the others froze. Jason's pacing had taken him straight up to Gabriel's chair. He stood there now, staring down with fire in his eyes.

"Tell me about my mother."

The seconds ticked by, too many to count. At first, Gabriel was simply speechless. Then he shook his head slowly, weighing each word. "Jason...I don't know anything about your mother."

Wrong answer.

Jason took a step back and something between them died.

"I went to the apartment," he said softly. "I saw the initials." His eyes burned with anger as the words he'd been keeping in for so long finally came pouring out. "*E.H.* Who was she??"

There was a quiet pause, then Gabriel let out a sigh.

"E.H. stands for Elaine Hobbs."

The name rang out between them.

"She was your mother."

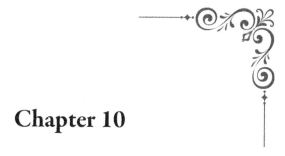

Chapter 10

The four of them sat in the living room for ages, but no one dared to speak. No one dared to even move. They were simply frozen, listening as the fire crackled.

Then finally Jason took a step back.

"Elaine..."

The name barely made it past his lips. It was one he'd been searching for all his life, yet now that it was in his possession he couldn't think what to do with it. He turned to his father instead.

"How could you not tell me?"

There wasn't even much anger in his voice—they were somewhere past that. And to be fair, he had a point. No matter how many times Gabriel had tried to shield or protect his son in the past, one thing remained consistent. He was always honest. And of all the things for him to withhold?

Gabriel leaned back in his chair, closing his eyes in a moment of sheer exhaustion. "You went to the apartment," he repeated quietly, raking his fingers through his hair. "How many times have I debated taking you, and in the end you go there on your own."

Angel shot him a look, but said nothing. Aria was wishing she'd gone back to the dorms.

"Dad," Jason's voice rang out sharp between them. "How could you not tell me?"

Plenty of anger there now. And hurt. Lots of hurt.

Gabriel gazed up at him, sad as the children had ever seen. "I didn't tell you because there was nothing to tell. I went to the apartment. I saw the initials. I thought it would only be a matter of time before I tracked her down...but I couldn't."

Jason shook his head, refusing to be dissuaded. "But you knew her name—"

"There was a woman's name on the lease," Gabriel interrupted softly, "Elaine Hobbs. Right there next to Wyatt's. The day after we brought you home, I started looking. Did everything I could to find her. I checked hospitals, DMV records, birth certificates for every county in England."

Jason stood in front of him, frozen with an uncertain expression. "...you checked?"

"Of course I checked," Gabriel replied gently. "Even if I hadn't found the initials, I would have launched a search. The woman was your biological mother. Wyatt had no will. I had no legal claim to you. And as much as I would have wanted—"

Angel flashed him a quick look and he caught himself.

"The longer you stayed with me, the more I lost the ability to be objective," he admitted. "I had Carter run her through the system. Had Julian and Natasha work with trackers to see what they could find. I even called the Minister of Immigration at the Home Office to see if there were any records. A woman by that name has never lived in London. Or Italy. Or America. Or France."

Aria was clutching the edge of her seat, feeling so light-headed she had to remind herself to breathe. She had only distant memories of the time when Jason joined their family. Most of those memories were of the adults talking in hushed voices, while she and Benji were sent to play outside.

She had no idea they'd been searching. She had no idea how Jason would feel about it now.

"So you were trying to return me," he finally managed, eyes searching the floor as he tried to make sense of it all. "Trying to take—"

"I was relieved."

Jason's eyes lifted in confusion and Gabriel gave him a little smile.

"I didn't want to give you back, put you in the hands of some random woman. I wanted to keep you. I wanted this place to be your home. I wanted you to be my son."

That same uncertain emotion swept over him before Jason's eyes hardened once more.

"Then maybe you didn't check hard enough."

"Jason," Angel chided sharply. "Your father did absolutely everything he could."

There was something about the way she said 'your father' that was as much a comfort as it was a warning. But Jason could heed neither. His head was trapped in a burnt-out apartment.

"Everything except tell me," he said suddenly, turning to Gabriel once more. "You knew my mother's name. You found her initials. How could you *possibly* not tell me?"

Gabriel let out a quiet sigh, then pushed to his feet. "For thirteen years, those letters haunted me. I used to live in fear, staring at the front door, thinking she might show up one day and take you away. Thirteen years with no answers, no closure, just those bloody letters carved into the wall. I guess... I guess I wanted to spare you from that."

Jason stood there for a moment longer, looking like some part of him was about to break. Then he spun on his heel and stormed from the living room.

"That wasn't your decision to make."

The front door slammed a moment later.

Aria glanced around nervously as a heavy silence enveloped the room. Angel and Gabriel didn't seem to notice it. They had been raised in such vacuums. But she was finding it hard to breathe. After a few seconds of restless fidgeting, she spoke up in a trembling voice.

"That could have gone worse. I mean...the cottage is still standing."
That's more than you can say when my family fights.

The adults looked over at her slowly, like they'd almost forgotten she was there. Angel looked faintly amused, but Gabriel was unreadable. It was impossible to tell what was going on behind those green eyes. But he had to be hurting. And it tore at her heart.

"He's just in shock," she continued tentatively. "He's going to come round—"

Gabriel waved her silent with a sad smile. "You don't need to apologize for him—he's right to be angry." He looked like he was going to say more, then shook his head. "And you were a good friend to stay with him tonight."

Aria bowed her head with a blush, wondering what Natasha might have told him. Wondering if he knew that she and his son were more than just good friends.

"You should get back to the dorms," he continued, glancing out the window at the darkened school. "I don't know how you snuck out...but sneak back in the same way."

She blushed again, quickly pushing to her feet. The trip down memory lane might have been mildly excruciating, but at least it had saved her from an interrogation about that night.

After giving both Gabriel and Angel a quick hug, she hurried to the door—wondering which tatù to use when climbing back up the wall. She'd just settled on a set of panther ink she'd come to favor when she turned around suddenly, one hand still clutching the door.

"Uncle Gabriel...why did you tell my dad what we talked about in the Oratory that day?"

She certainly wasn't complaining. The only reason she'd gotten to go on a mission to New York was because Gabriel had somehow managed to change her father's mind. But it did strike her as strange. He would usually speak with her mother. The two had a special connection.

Angel laughed shortly and pushed to her feet, going to salvage whatever was left of the coffee-maker, while Gabriel lifted his eyebrows with a faint smile.

"You want me to tell *your mother* to let her teenage daughter leave the nest and fight crime?"

He shook his head and returned his eyes to the window.

"Devon married Rae. He gets the honor of telling her things like that."

THE NEXT DAY, THE GANG attended classes as usual. Or rather, some of them did. One of their members was suspiciously absent—holed away in his dorm, carving the letters 'E.H.' into the wall.

Aria pretended she didn't notice and dodged the others' questions about what had happened back at the cottage. For the most part, it worked. The only time she had trouble was in Dorian's history class, when she and Alexander found themselves sitting alone in the back of the room.

"Where's your boyfriend?" he asked as the rest of class began talking amongst themselves.

Aria's eyes flashed up, but she kept her cool. "Probably laid up in bed recovering from a tiger attack. Why?" She glared at him across the desks. "Would you like to talk about that?"

He stared at her a moment, then chuckled and began unloading his supplies. "You know, my sister was right about you. You're hard to dislike."

Aria's head jerked up in surprise. "Sofia said that?"

After their confrontation the other night, she wouldn't have thought the girl was a fan. Then again, they shared a secret. And that was a difficult bond to break.

"Mmm-hmm." Alexander pulled out a piece of paper and dropped two pencils onto his desk. "At first, I didn't agree. Now, I'm not so sure."

She rolled her eyes and snatched a pencil for herself. "If I'm coming off as *likable* to you, then I'm clearly doing something wrong."

His eyes flickered to hers with a fleeting grin. "Well, I wouldn't call you *very* likable. Then again, it helps when you take your top off."

The pencil snapped in half.

"Are you serious?" she hissed, almost forgetting to keep her voice down. Dorian's attention drifted their way and she forced a quick smile. "You walk up on me kissing some other guy, claw him to pieces with your demented tiger claws, and *still*, for reasons unknown to man, he decides to save you. All that...and you're going to sit there making these jokes at me?!"

There was a pause.

"...who says I'm joking?"

THAT'S IT!

"Miss Wardell!" Dorian's voice suddenly sounded from across the room, and those students sitting closest turned their way. "I believe I asked you *not* to light my classroom on fire?"

Aria looked down with a start to see smoke rising from her hands. She extinguished them quickly, sliding them into her pockets for good measure.

Alexander watched the entire thing with a smirk. "Speaking of Jason," he began innocently, "I couldn't help but notice the whole kissing thing felt...rather new. Maybe even the first time?"

She blushed in spite of herself, flashing an incriminating look at Benji. Normally, the guy would be shamelessly eavesdropping with his ink. However, given the fact that, at the moment, he was sitting across from a beautiful and equally passive aggressive shifter, he was rather distracted.

Alexander smirked again.

"I thought so. And your little band of warriors...they don't know?"

They certainly WILL if you keep talking about it!

"I don't see how that's any of your business," she answered coolly, picking up both halves of her pencil and melding them together with a flick of her hand. "I don't even see why you'd care, given that I'm apparently not *that* likable."

"Things change." He gave her a smile, flashing every one of his pearly teeth. "*People* change."

She pulled in a steadying breath, trying to control her temper. "What's that supposed to mean?"

"It means most new relationships don't tend to last. And that's when things are easy." His eyes flickered around the classroom. "This place doesn't strike me as very easy."

She tilted her head with a cold smile. "Well, maybe he's up for the challenge."

Alexander smiled back evenly. "We'll see."

THE REST OF THE CLASS period was like slow-walking backwards through a nightmare. Aria did everything she could to keep her head above water, but every word Alexander said had wormed its way deep inside her mind. By the time the bell rang, she was in a full-on tailspin.

Were she and Jason doomed from the start? Two seconds after they decided to get into a relationship, one of them almost bled out on the grass. They hadn't talked about it since. She wasn't even sure he remembered they'd done it. And why did it take them so long to get together in the first place? They'd known each other since they were five years old. But it wasn't until this year—

"Arie."

She looked up to see Benji standing beside her desk, staring down with a strange expression on his face. Alexander was already gone. She wondered how long he'd been standing there.

"Class is over. You okay?"

The rest of the classroom was empty. Even Dorian had wandered off to the faculty lounge to refill his coffee. She crammed her things into her bag then leapt to her feet.

"Yeah—sorry. Just lost track of things." She flashed a quick smile, hoping he wouldn't overthink it. "How did things go with Sofia?"

Sure enough he let out a sigh, rolling his eyes.

"She isn't speaking to me. The *whole* time. Not one word."

Aria forced a laugh as they swept through the desks. "What did you expect?" she quipped. "One second you're playing footsie with her in history class, the next you're cutting her out of our top secret plan. I'd be pissed, too."

Rather predictably, Benji ignored all the relevant information and focused on a single detail. "I was not playing *footsie*." He spat out the word like it was something foul.

"Uh-huh."

They breezed into the hall, only to find it in full swing. The campus itself may have still been on a bogus lock-down, but the teachers were making every effort to keep things running the same as usual. Benji headed towards the science building but Aria stayed where she was, hesitant to follow.

After a few steps he glanced back, realizing she wasn't with him for the first time.

"Are you coming?"

Am I?

The practical part of her said 'yes', but a dozen half-formed questions raced through her mind and she found herself backing away.

"I'm going back to the dorms—feeling a little sick. You'll tell Professor Galton?"

Benji nodded, looking a little confused. "Yeah, sure."

He was still staring as she raced in the opposite direction—heading not towards the women's dorm, but to the men's. Those questions weren't going to answer themselves.

And she'd been waiting long enough.

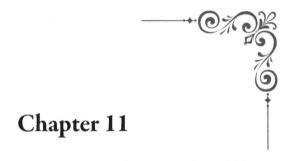

Chapter 11

Several years ago, Rae Kerrigan had picked up a handy set of ink that allowed her to unlock any door with a touch of her hand. While she and her friends had jokingly complained it took all the fun out of cracking open a bank vault, the real problem was yet to come.

Because the day Aria turned sixteen, she picked up the ink as well.

Open—NOW!

It was hard to work under the best of circumstances but, like most forms of magic, it helped when there was a strong emotion behind it. Right now, Aria had that in spades.

The door not only cracked open, it swung right off the hinges—flying into the room with a crash. A muffled profanity rose up from all the dust and she froze guiltily in the frame—wondering whether it was better to cut and run, leaving him to blame it on a particularly aggressive wind.

Then she saw the papers.

What the ...?

The normally tidy room was completely submerged in a literal forest of print-outs. In some places, they covered the floor a foot deep. What they were and how Jason had possibly gotten them all there was a complete mystery—one that temporarily derailed her interrogation.

"Jase?"

There was movement in the corner. A hand emerged from the sea of paper, waving weakly before pushing aside the heavy door. His face appeared a moment later, flushed and breathless.

"Oh, it's you." A painful smile filled his face as he extracted himself gingerly from the pile. "Of course it's you—who else comes into a room like that?"

"What are you doing?" she asked slowly, bending down to pick up a stray piece. It read like a medical file. Name, age, location. "Eliza Habberton? Who is this?"

Jason paused with a flash of embarrassment, then pushed to his feet—gesturing down at the pile. "It could be my mother." He picked up the door and replaced it on the frame—hopefully slightly secure.

Aria's eyes widened before she glanced back down at the page. "Mortician's assistant?"

"Well, probably not *that* one."

The page slipped from Aria's fingers as she slowly looked over the room. A sense of sudden understanding swept over her, followed by a heartache that tugged plaintively at her chest.

"All these women..." she murmured, shifting the colossus with her foot. "You're looking through *all* these women..."

Jason flushed again at the astronomical odds, then tried to rally.

"What's more likely—that the woman suddenly vanished from the face of the earth, or that she just changed her name?" He grabbed up a random handful of papers, shaking them. "I read somewhere that when people do that, they tend to keep their same initials. These women are all in the right age bracket and come from a heritage that could technically produce someone who looks like me." The names fell to the floor as he looked at the mountain around him a bit hopelessly. "I thought I'd start there..."

Aria pursed her lips, trying very hard not to smile. It wasn't enough that the papers covered the floor—they were stacked upon the beds and the shelves as well. There didn't seem to be any sort of order to them, except that they all detailed women with the initials E and H.

"And you're making progress?"

He shot her a rueful grin.

"...they were better organized before."

A flush of shame warmed Aria's cheeks as she stared down at the broken door. There she was, raging in unannounced to question him about a high school romance that may or may not be happening, and all the while Jason was on a quest to find his long-lost mother.

"I'm sorry for..." She trailed off. "I'll just let you get back to it—"

He caught her by the hand.

"I'm sorry I left you with Alexander today," he murmured. "I didn't remember until halfway through the class. And...I'm sorry about last night, too." His cheeks flushed as he bowed his head. "I didn't mean to storm out like that."

"I understand why you did." She settled tentatively on a stack of papers, patting the place beside her. "You know...your dad understands, too. I think he feels really bad about it."

Jason hesitated before taking a seat. "Yeah, well...he should."

She shot him a sideways glance, not wanting to push the wrong buttons but unable to let something like that go at the same time. "...should he?"

Jason shot her a quick look and she held up her hands.

"Honestly, Jase," she pressed gently, "would you have done anything different?" The friends were eternally tender to each other and blind to each other's faults, but at the same time they didn't shy away from hard truths. "If you had a kid in the same situation, and no matter what you tried, you *couldn't* find the answers that he needed...wouldn't you have done the exact same thing?"

A flash of anger shot through Jason's eyes.

"But it wasn't his decision. I wasn't his kid."

Aria smiled patiently, shaking her head. "You don't mean that."

There was a defiant pause, then Jason leaned back against the bed with a sigh. Pushing tangled waves of blonde hair out of his face.

"No, I don't." He kicked half-heartedly at the mountain of papers. "This is a mess. And I used up half the toner in the library printing it all out. Why did I ever think this was going to work?"

"Because it might." Aria groped around in the pile, then pulled out a name. "Elizabeth Harcourt. Thirty-seven. Works at an animal preserve in Kent deworming African baboons." She waved it hopefully between them. "You think that's her?"

There was a beat of silence.

"It does not say that."

"It might."

"There are no African baboons in Kent."

"There *might* be."

The two friends leaned back against the bed, laughing softly. It was easier to find the humor in things when they were together. Easier to pretend like the problems facing them might have actual solutions. That they might actually get the answers to all those endless questions.

"How were you going to keep all this from Benji?" she finally asked, nudging the pile with her toe. It was stacked on the cheetah's bed as well, and had completely submerged his computer.

Jason lifted his shoulders in a shrug. "I was going to say it was spring cleaning."

Ridiculous as it might sound, it wasn't a bad idea. The boy might have eyes like a hawk, but he could also been impressively unobservant when he deemed something unworthy of his time. At the word 'cleaning' he was sure to tune out entirely.

"*Spring* cleaning?" she pressed with a smile. "It's coming up on Christmas."

Jason shook his head with an affectionate grin. "Yeah, well, the guy's a loon. At any rate, he's been a little distracted lately."

All at once, the image came back to her. Two sets of legs crossed beneath the desks. Two heads bent together, smiling at the same shared joke.

"Yeah, he has." Aria slid down a few inches, crossing her arms over her chest. "You should have seen him with Sofia today." She shook her head in disgust. "As if he could even be considering that sort of thing at a time like this."

Jason shot her a quick look, then dropped his gaze. "Would that be so crazy?" he asked lightly, glancing from the corner of his eyes. "To be thinking about it?"

She froze, staring down at her hands. "That depends."

The corners of his lips twitched. "On what?"

She forced herself to look at him, half-ready to bolt from the room. "On how much you remember about that night."

For a second, they just stared. Every muscle on high alert, she was leaning towards the door without even thinking. Then he took her by the wrist, easing her closer.

"I remember everything..."

Before she knew what was happening, she was sitting on his lap—straddling him with her ankles locked behind his waist. She hadn't planned on moving. She hadn't even done most of it herself. A few skillful tugs of his hands and they were suddenly together.

"You thought I didn't remember?" he asked softly, gazing up at her. "This whole time, you thought it was just you?"

She flushed and bowed her head, her hair spilling down.

"It would be understandable," she murmured. "I know we keep looping back to it, but you did almost *die* that night, Jason. I'm actually a little surprised—"

"—a little surprised I remember asking you to be my girlfriend?" That same crooked smile tugged at the corners of his mouth. "Arie...that's not the sort of thing you can forget."

She was smiling now, too, reaching up to twirl a lock of his hair.

"As I recall, you didn't exactly ask me to be your girlfriend," she answered coyly. "I mean, you never actually said the words."

He leaned into her hand, pretending not to. "I didn't figure you to be so traditional."

She bit her lip, trying to control her expression. "Oh yes, very traditional. I'd actually prefer that you ask my father first."

An actual shudder ran through his shoulders as he leaned against the bed, considering the possibility for the first time. "Now *there's* a chilling thought..."

She let out a laugh, swatting his shoulders. "I'm kidding. And besides—my dad loves you."

"He loves me like a nephew," Jason clarified. "He would *not* love me dating his only daughter. Trust me. He's not going to love anyone who signs up for that."

She shrugged daintily, glancing at her nails. "Well, like I said, you never actually signed up—"

He caught her face in both hands, eyes twinkling with a secret smile. "Aria Wardell...will you be my girlfriend?"

Her skin warmed and her heart skipped unevenly in her chest. Not for the first time, she was suddenly glad he didn't have a shifter's advanced senses. Otherwise it would be a dead giveaway.

That being said, he seemed to know anyway. The mischief faded from his smile, leaving it softer and more serious. As their eyes locked, a thumb came up to stroke the side of her cheek.

"...will you?"

She thrilled in a moment in silent bliss, then lifted a casual shoulder. "If you like. You don't have to be so formal about it..."

That's when he threw her into the air.

"What—"

She smashed onto the bed a second later, breathless with peals of laughter, sending hundreds of papers fluttering towards the ceiling. Before they could land Jason jumped on top of her, pinning her casually to the mattress while shaking his head with a punishing smile.

"Oh I'm sorry, were you making a joke?"

She tried to shake her head, but she was laughing too hard. He took full advantage of the moment to begin tickling her mercilessly—anchoring her to the bed with his knees.

"Did that strike you as a moment to be funny?"

She struggled and writhed, still gasping for breath, but could do nothing to shake him. She tried to use her powers, but he pinned her wrists securely above her head.

"Now...is that a yes?" he asked sternly. "You're not the only traditionalist around here. I need to hear a formal answer."

The tickling came to a pause, leaving her flushed and grinning.

"That's a yes."

His eyes twinkled as his free hand brushed a lock of hair from her face.

"That's really good news," he said softly. "Because I *have* been thinking about it. And there's something I've been wanting to do for a long time..."

He leaned closer, hovering just an inch away from her face, but suddenly paused. The muscles in his arms went rigid as his eyes flashed up to her face.

Tell me you actually want this. His thoughts rang out loud and clear, betraying a fear he'd never dream of saying out loud. *Tell me you want this as much as I do.*

Her heart melted as she stared up at him, never knowing it was possible to feel so protective and desired all at the same time. She pulled a hand free, trailing her fingers down the side of his face.

"Kiss me."

That was the last of the talking.

The moment the two of them came together, there was no pulling them apart. Their bodies melted together like they'd been designed for the very purpose, like they'd been waiting years just for the chance. His hand slipped into her hair. Her legs wrapped around his waist. When he reached tentatively for the base of her shirt, she slipped it off without a second thought.

"Just tell me," he panted, kissing the side of her neck, "just tell me if you want to stop."

Her head was spinning, her heart was pounding, and for the life of her she couldn't take her hands off him. But his words lodged somewhere deep inside her brain.

When DID she want to stop?

Unlike Jason, unlike Benji...she'd never actually slept with someone before. Yes, she'd fooled around with guys, snuck in and out of her share of dorm rooms. Things had even gotten a little serious once, but Benji didn't like the guy so it was over before it began.

But Jason Alden...? That was a whole different level.

She nodded quickly, realizing he was waiting for a reply, but found herself physically incapable of putting any distance between their bodies. His tongue was in her mouth. Her hands were fiddling with the top of his pants. She was about a second away from taking things to a place she might not have been ready for, when the sound of footsteps pounded towards the room.

"*Crap!*"

They leapt away from each other at the same time—flying to opposite sides of the room. It was a rare moment that she wouldn't have been using her fennec fox tatù, but since ripping his door off the hinges she'd yet to switch back.

She scrambled to button her shirt while Jason smoothed down his clothes. His hair looked like she'd attacked it with a butter knife, but there was no helping that now. Distracted as they were, they only had a few seconds before—

"Bloody hell!"

The door flew open, miraculously saying on its hinges, and Benji stepped into the frame, staring around the room like he couldn't believe his eyes. There was a split second where she and Jason froze, barely breathing, then he threw down his school bag atop the ocean of papers littering the floor.

"What's all this?"

If he'd been paying more attention, he might have noticed the way both his friends let out a breath at the same time. He might have seen the fact that Aria had mismatched several buttons, and Jason had a giant tear running up the side of his shirt. But he didn't. He was too busy reading about Emma Holt—a thirty-nine-year-old receptionist at a Manchester hotel.

Jason raked back his hair, still trying to catch his breath. "Uh...spring cleaning?"

"Oh." Benji looked at him for an endless moment. "Yeah, that makes sense."

Aria would have laughed if she wasn't still having a mild heart attack from what had almost just happened. And no, she wasn't thinking about when Benji had burst inside.

"I thought you went back to your dorm," Benji said sarcastically. "Feeling better?"

She forced a tight smile, perching awkwardly on the side of the bed. "You know we can't leave him unsupervised," she mumbled, trying her best to avoid Jason's eyes. "There's no telling what trouble he might get in to."

Jason pursed his lips, staring pointedly out the window, while Benji flopped onto his bed with a laugh. "Yeah, that's actually what I had in mind..."

The others turned to him at the same time.

"What do you mean?" Aria asked with a frown.

Benji held up a finger, finishing off a text. No sooner had his phone dinged than the door opened again and Lily swept gracefully into the room.

"No need for the message, I'm already here."

"Great," Jason muttered, folding his arms awkwardly in front of his chest. "We should just open the door and invite everyone inside..."

"What's with the papers?" The psychic knelt down and picked one up, holding it by her fingertips. She scanned quickly, then looked up in surprise. "Are you thinking of going to medical school?"

"Of course not," Jason snapped. But he confiscated the doctor's file and put it with a pile of other hopefuls on his desk. "I'm just...cleaning. You know how it is."

She lifted her eyebrows with a knowing smile. "Yes, I do. Was Arie helping you?"

Jason froze on the spot, still clutching a random handful of papers. "Was...I didn't...excuse me?"

"With the cleaning," Lily clarified innocently.

Aria shot her a death look, while Jason turned the color of spoiled milk.

"Why are you guys here?" she asked rather sharply.

"*I* happen to live here," Benji answered without missing a beat. "And I texted Lily, because the four of us have business to sort out and I figured we might as well do it now."

Aria paused, curious for the first time. "What business?"

"Don't tell me you've forgotten already," Benji teased, eyes lighting up with that look of mischief she knew so well. "We're going on a little patrol tonight..."

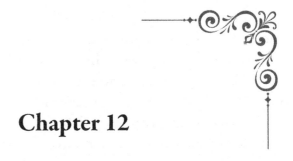

Chapter 12

Throughout their parents' years of service, many phrases slipped into the vocabulary of a spy. Things like 'lying low' and 'waiting for the heat to die down'. Aria and her friends may have found themselves on the other side of the law virtually every day that week, but no one had ever seen fit to employ them as spies. Perhaps it was for that reason that they went right back out again that night.

"You know," Lily panted, dropping down onto the grass, "we should really invest in a rope ladder or something. Maybe an invisible pulley system going down the outside of the tower?"

Aria landed beside her, straightening up from a roll. "Or we could just buy Madame Elpis some earplugs."

Both girls were lacking the official PC spy-wear they so craved, but they'd made do the best they could. Black leggings, dark camisoles, and skin-tight sweaters that zipped all the way to their chins.

Aria had even tentatively suggested the idea of a beanie, but the only one she possessed was a strange tie-dyed monstrosity from elementary school which she silently put back on the shelf.

They darted across the moonlit lawn, sticking as close as they could to the shadows. About a hundred paces away, both Benji and Jason were making their way out of Joist Hall. Given their rather lax housemaster, they didn't necessarily need to jump out the top story window. But a feeling of adventure had seized them as well and they were halfway down, dangling from the stone.

Aria switched into an owl tatù with a grin, listening in on their conversation.

"—*terrible idea. Why do I always let you talk me into these kinds of things*—"

"—*stop complaining. At least we caught the stereo before it could fall*—"

The girls stopped at their meeting spot beneath the trees, watching from a distance as the two tiny silhouettes abandoned the idea of a climb and dropped silently to the earth. They were so busy congratulating each other that they didn't see a third silhouette peek its head out of one of the lower windows before hurling itself to the ground.

"Uh-oh," Lily whispered with a grin. "There's going to be trouble."

Aria stood bolt upright beside her, planting her hands on her hips with a furious scowl.

"As well there should be," she hissed, watching as her little brother joined the others and started heading their way across the grass. "Why does he always think he's invited?"

"...because he *is* invited."

"And why exactly is that?" she demanded. "He's young, he doesn't have powers, and he regularly makes me want to set myself on fire!"

"...he's your brother."

"Like I said."

The trio of boys joined them a second later. The others had already forgiven the intrusion and James was wedged between them with a breathless grin—a jet black beanie stuck over his hair.

"Hey, guys! So what's the plan?"

Aria glanced at the beanie before her eyes narrowed with a glare. "We were going to do a little late-night patrol around some of the cottages," she answered rudely. "But I don't seem to remember anyone inviting you—"

"We'd be *happy* for the help," Lily said pointedly, throwing an arm around his shoulders. In times of sibling conflict, she was usually the one to step up in the boy's defense. "Come on, James."

He flashed a smug grin at his sister before following the rest of them through the trees.

Sometime that morning, Carter had ceased his need to punish the children with theatrics and called off the constant patrols. Everyone who was in the infirmary that night knew Alexander was the one who'd attacked Jason in the woods—there was no longer a point in keeping agents up at all hours of the day and night searching for the person who did it. Ironically enough, it was an agent himself who'd convinced him. When Carter had found Michael Jeffreys training in the Oratory the night before, instead of watching the woods, he acknowledged the absurdity of it and relented.

The investigation into the murder of Professor Dorf still continued, but most of that was happening either off campus or behind closed doors.

...or with a group of teenagers in the woods that night.

"You know, all of this is based on a pretty big assumption," James murmured, stepping quietly as they headed towards the cottages. "That Dorian was the target, instead of Dorf."

It was a good point, though none of them was saying it. It also happened to be one of Aria's least favorite things about her brother—his annoying tendency to point out things like facts.

"So leave," she said coldly. "If this is such a waste of time."

Benji flashed her a look, and she amended with a sigh.

"What I meant to say is...*please* leave."

The others chuckled under their breath, but James didn't seem to mind. It seemed by now to be a foregone conclusion that he and his sister would be locked in a mortal struggle until the end of time. He held back a tree branch for the others before snapping it into her face.

"I'm serious," he continued calmly. "What makes you think it's Professor Locke?"

"A lack of other options," Jason replied. "It either was Dorf, a man with no enemies who barely ever left the school—"

"In which case this is all over," Benji interjected.

"—or it was someone else. They went to the history building. That means someone was either looking for Dorf or Uncle Luke. And while our parents might have a thousand enemies, I can't see anyone attacking them in the middle of campus. Let alone in a hand-to-hand fight."

Aria nodded sharply, flashing her brother a dirty glare. "Hence the patrol."

"Yeah, but Dorian doesn't teach history," James insisted. "Or at least he didn't at the time of the murder. How could anyone know he'd be promoted to fill the spot?"

The others shared a quick glance. In their eagerness to do something proactive, they occasionally forgot about those pesky facts themselves.

"Yes, but he was never supposed to be a librarian," Lily added suddenly, latching on to this point. "He used to teach history at his old school. If anyone from that part of his life held a grudge and knew he'd come to teach at Guilder, it makes sense that they'd start by looking there."

James nodded, mulling it over. "So are you guys planning a trip to Sussex?"

Aria looked up at him in surprise. "Why we would do that?"

"Sussex is lame," Benji added matter-of-factly.

James rolled his eyes, stopping with the rest of them when they came to the edge of the trees. "You guys just said that if the target really was Dorian, then the attacker is someone from his old life. Which was in Sussex." They blinked back at him. "Do I need to spell this out for you?"

Benji and Aria shared a quick glance before he shoved James with a playful grin.

"We're just messing with you, kid. Of *course* we're going to Sussex."

...we are?

"We were just waiting until all the drama died down at school," Jason added quickly.

...we are!

"Don't be an idiot," Aria nodded stiffly. "We were always planning to go."

Mental note: go to Sussex.

The boy nodded quickly and turned back to the cottages, squinting in the darkness. Benji and Jason stood on either side, exchanging a swift glance behind his head, while Lily melted back to Aria's side. Trying not to grin as she whispered in her ear.

"*That's* why James is always invited along..."

CONSIDERING THE LEGACY of their parents, the friends didn't know much when it came to surveillance. There were things their families talked about, and things they didn't. Most of what they were planning for the night was based on movies and spy shows on TV. It would be safest to simply watch from a distance, they'd decided. Rely on Arie and Benji to listen in. Keep an eye on the rest of campus for anything unusual. It was going to be easy. No one would ever know.

That's when they saw the three shifters hiding in the trees.

As it turned out, they weren't the only ones on patrol...

You've GOT to be kidding me!

"Hey!" Aria hissed.

The trio noticed them at the same time, jumping in alarm before rolling their eyes and turning together in a quick huddle. Sofia was gesturing desperately back to the dorms, whispering under her breath. But Alexander shook his head, marching arrogantly through the trees.

"Well, hello there," he greeted them with a twisted smile. "And what brings you fine people out this evening?"

The friends were nothing but annoyed, but James stepped forward with a gasp.

"What are *you* doing here!" he demanded, not bothering to hide his emotions.

Aria stared at him in surprise, then realized the last time he'd seen Alexander the shifter was being held between two guards in the middle of the infirmary. The time immediately before that Jason had been bleeding, she'd been sobbing, and the tiger been about two seconds away from ripping a lightning-wielding Benji in half. Needless to say, James had *not* gotten over it.

"It's all right," she soothed, placing a hand on his arm. "He was out with us the other night when we realized the target might have been Dorian. He knew we were going to keep an eye on things. I just didn't know he and the others would be patrolling, too."

She'd expected this to help but James ripped his arm away, whirling around in shock.

"He was out with you the other night?!" he repeated in dismay. "What are you talking about, Arie? Why are you even speaking to him?!"

Alexander raised his eyebrows with the hint of a genuine smile. "Feisty kid."

"Shut up!" James cried before the others could leap in themselves. "You shouldn't even be here, all right? The only reason you're still at this school is because my friends and I aren't talking."

He took a step closer, staring at the tiger with a total lack of fear.

"And that could change at any time."

Aria slipped into a strength tatù without realizing, placing a hand squarely in between them. But Alexander only smiled. For once, there was nothing menacing about it. In fact, it was borderline affectionate. The smile that only an older sibling could ever truly master.

"You're a good brother," he said softly. "And a good friend."

James stopped short, completely thrown off balance. Standing behind him the friends froze in unison, waiting for the other shoe to drop. Only Sofia smiled, bowing her head quickly to hide it.

"I'm not trying to do anything to upset your sister," Alexander continued calmly. "And I'm highly aware that my position here is at the mercy of your friends. The only reason the three of us are out tonight is to try and limit the faculty homicides at Guilder this year to one."

There was a beat of silence.

"Oh—like you care about Professor Locke?" Lily snapped, arms folded tightly across her chest. "I agree with James—they should just leave."

"When *I'm* the one suspected of murdering his predecessor, yes, I care very much what happens to Professor Locke," Alexander fired back. "And why do you care about motives anyway? In the end, we all want the same thing."

"I care because there are limits to how far we'll take things," she answered coolly. "We know firsthand you have no limits. And that's not the kind of person we can trust."

He took a step closer, staring down with a sneer. "So don't trust me. You don't have to. The only thing you *have* to do is make sure that librarian isn't strangled in his sleep. And my friends and I can help you with that."

"Back off," Jason said quietly, eyeing the distance between them. He might not have been a shifter, but the guy's power was as deadly as any other. Maybe even more. "Only warning."

Alexander gritted his teeth, trying in vain to rein in that violent temper. But Lily wasn't making it easy. For every inch he retreated, she made up for it tenfold.

"We already decided—"

"And it wasn't your decision to make, princess." His eyes flashed as they swept over the whole group. "Now, who do you think stands a better chance of catching this guy? Three people with no advanced sensory ink whatsoever, or three shifters—"

"There are *five* of us," Benji corrected coldly, coming to Lily's side. It took quite a bit to strain his patience, but Alexander had crossed that line long ago. The sight of him so close to Lily was enough to send him over the edge. "But only three of us would get expelled if we're caught out here, so why don't you and your friends get back inside before I forget to lower my voice."

Sofia flinched, but for once he wasn't looking. The silent treatment in history class, combined with everything else that had happened the last few days, seemed to have cooled whatever affections might have been stirring.

Alexander took a step closer, cocking his head with a grin. "You know, if I didn't know any better I'd swear you were *hoping* someone attacks the little teacher tonight. Just so you can get the credit for dragging the guy in."

Aria's fingers clenched as she prepared to literally punch the grin right off the guy's face. But Benji only smiled, shaking his head like he was attempting to teach an obstinate child a lesson.

"See, that right there is the difference between you and me. I'd never wish for bad things to happen to good people. I'll simply be ready if they do."

A muscle twitched in Alexander's jaw.

"And you think I'm one of those bad things?"

Benji's lips curved in a slow smile, the center of his eyes flickering with an electric glow. "I think, one way or another, we're about to find out."

Just like that, the two groups were divided—charged with the kind of tension that had led to that first confrontation all those nights ago. Eric's arms flexed with anticipation, like he was already summoning the bear within, while tiny sparks began dripping from Benji's hands into the grass.

"Ben—*stop*," Jason commanded.

He hadn't sacrificed all credibility with his father only to have a repeat of the same damning fight. A chill swept over the clearing, almost like someone had thrown a curtain over the stars and moon, as his own tatù rose to the surface. He struggled to control it, holding Benji back.

"What did you expect?" Benji murmured, almost to himself. A faint glow was circling around his body, flooding from those electric eyes. "He did it once, he'll do it again."

Jason flinched as a shock traveled through his friend's body, but didn't relax his grip.

"You swore to me—"

"I swore to protect you a long time before that," Benji interrupted swiftly. In his mind, there was no decision. The decision had already been made. All that was left to do was pick sides. "Arie."

He said it with no hesitation, already anticipating her reply. He didn't see the conflicted look that washed over her face—the way Jason turned and the two of them locked eyes.

They're going to fight, she said telepathically, trying to win him over. *You know it's going to happen—there's no stopping it. All we can do now is make sure we're on the winning side.*

Jason stared at her a moment longer, then shook his head.

"Lily," he murmured, "think you can work that ink again?"

Her dark eyes flickered over the clearing but, whether or not she'd be able to freeze those tempers before they boiled over, she didn't seem inclined to try. Instead she reached into her vest and extracted a pair of silver knives she'd gotten for her birthday, giving them a ready twirl.

"You promised," Sofia whispered, staring at the back of her brother's head. The words barely carried past the next tree, but he heard them. "You promised me no more fights."

A flicker of hesitation tightened Alexander's features, but he kept his eyes on Benji.

"And you promised me they were different."

"Enough!" Jason shouted. "This isn't happening, all right? It's not why we're here!"

Be that as it may, it was clearly happening.

"James, go back to Joist," Aria commanded.

He threw her a disbelieving glare. "You've got to be kidding—"

"*Now*, Jamie."

"Don't worry about James," Benji breathed, lifting his hands. "This will only take a minute."

Three cries pierced the night as the boys lunged at each other. But one noise overpowered them all—the sound of shattering glass echoing in the darkness.

Both Alexander and Benji froze just inches away from each other. Then they turned with the rest of them towards the tiny cottages dotting the periphery of the school.

"Dorian," Aria whispered, paling in horror. "That came from his house."

They were on the move a second later, all eight of them sprinting out from the safety of the trees. The lights were off, save for a faint glow coming from one of the windows, but there was no time to make a plan. Without a second's pause Aria kicked down the front door and they raced into the house, hands raised, powers flashing, sliding to a stop in front of the kitchen...

...where Dorian stood with a broom and a pail.

"Aria?" he gasped in shock, staring at the rest of them. A broken tea cup lay in pieces by his feet. "What on earth are you all doing here?"

A sudden silence swept over the room.

Aria's mouth fell open, but she couldn't think of a single word. The man dropped a glass, and next thing he knew his door had been kicked into the adjacent hall. There was no explaining it, no way to justify what the eight of them were doing out of bed let alone in his house. After a few seconds of awkward silence, she went out on a dangerous limb. She decided to tell the truth.

"...we were trying to save your life?"

Chapter 13

The door was fitted back on its hinges. The broken tea cup was swept up and the pieces were thrown into the bin. Two minutes later the eight teenagers were standing in a silent line in the living room—heads bowed, hands folded, bracing for whatever judgement might await.

"...well, this is awkward."

Aria peeked up through her lashes to see Dorian sitting in a chair across from them. His legs were folded, his fingers were drumming on the armrest, and it looked like he was trying very hard not to smile. When he caught her looking, he leaned down to catch her eye.

"My mother always warned me about touching broken porcelain, but I never realized it was a life-threatening offense."

The others shot each other a quick look, not knowing if they were expected to stay silent or laugh. At that point, Aria decided to go out on another limb...and lie.

"We were working on our research papers," she said lamely, hoping Jason and Alexander would take the hint and speak up. "Our question was about security—"

"And you were worried about mine?" Dorian interrupted lightly. "And you chose to investigate this security in the dead of night?"

The man might have been kind, but he was no pushover. In a strange way, he reminded her of Carter—able to see through to the heart of a matter no matter how hard they tried to hide.

"The killer snuck on to campus in the dead of night," she mumbled, avoiding his gaze. "It made sense to investigate how things were set up at the same time—"

"Aria," he cut her off again, more gently this time. "You were trying to save my life. Direct quote." He took off his glasses, staring up at her. "Tell me what's going on."

She glanced again at the others, but could think of nothing to do. They had been caught red-handed, and he clearly wasn't letting them go without telling the truth. The words hung in the air a moment before she took that final step off the ledge with a quiet sigh.

"We think someone's trying to kill you."

Dorian's eyes darted from one friend to the next, though his face showed no change. He simply nodded slowly, waiting for her to continue.

"The assassin who killed Professor Dorf...they went straight for the history building. But we don't think they got the person they were looking for. It was dark, it happened quickly, they could have easily come up from behind and assumed Dorf was someone else." She spoke quickly, staring down at her hands. "The only other teacher there was Uncle Luke, but we don't think that he would be the target either. Not considering, well...his other job."

Ironically enough, Luke Fodder's 'other job' was infinitely more dangerous than his time spent at Guilder teaching upper level history. The guy had fended off assassins too many times to count. But those times were usually in an industrial plant in Ukraine, or a crowded street fair in Greece. They very rarely happened in the rolling English countryside.

"...and you think that leaves me?"

The words fired out quickly, but it was impossible to tell whether Dorian was angry or not. If he was, he was doing a good job hiding it. But the question still remained.

"You taught history in Sussex," Benji said quietly, glancing up to meet his eyes. "If anyone knew you were coming here...it would be the first place they'd look."

Dorian flashed him a look and he bowed his head quickly, waiting for the axe to fall. But, as it turned out, he would be waiting for a long time.

The professor opened his mouth to answer then fell silent, staring somewhere past them with a vacant expression in his eyes. A second later he pushed to his feet, looking more troubled than he had at any point during their comical rescue.

"I thought I was being paranoid," he murmured, making his way to the window. "I didn't even think to file a report..."

Aria shot a look at the others, too breathless to speak. The man was quiet for a long moment before turning back to them with that same troubled frown.

"My office was broken in to yesterday," he said abruptly. "At least I think that's what happened." He gestured briskly around the cottage. "I don't know if you can tell, but I'm not exactly the most organized person in the world."

Aria followed his gaze with the hint of a smile. His blunt way of speaking reminded her of her parents, as did his tendency to take his work home with him. She'd been too anxious when they'd first arrived to notice, but every available inch of floor space was filled with a charming array of clutter. Everything from books, to boxes of clothes, to so many *more* books, she wondered why he didn't just ask if he could store some of them at the library. The office was a different story.

"What makes you think someone broke in?" she asked hesitantly, still wondering whether they were going to be drawn and quartered for trespassing.

"My car keys were missing," he answered quietly, speaking more to himself than to her. "As well as a few other things of little consequence. But the door was locked when I left, and open when I arrived. I didn't think much of it at the time. I found the keys on my desk this morning."

The friends shared another look, excited beyond belief but trying very hard to rein it in.

"And you didn't find any clues?" James blurted. "Any idea as to who might have done it?"

Dorian blinked and looked up suddenly, as if only then remembering they were there. His eyes swept down the line with something that bordered on affection.

"So let me get this straight." He gestured for them to take a seat. "All eight of you snuck out of your dorms to stand guard all night on the off chance that someone decided to attack me?"

Aria paused, not knowing what to say. "Uh...yeah, I guess."

Dorian's eyes twinkled and he nodded slowly. "And there was no plan besides if you saw something going wrong, you were going to attack and rescue me in the nick of time. Is that right?"

The friends blanched at the same time, feeling more than a little ridiculous. This time Aria nudged Jason, who self-consciously dug his toe into the carpet.

"Well, when you phrase it like that..."

Dorian laughed aloud, taking off his glasses and wiping them on his shirt. This time, the affection was undeniable. It lingered long after the laughter was over, softening into something more serious as he looked each one in the eye.

"Thank you. All of you." He chuckled again at their incredulous faces. "I mean it. While there were definitely a few flaws in execution...it's the thought that counts. Thank you—sincerely."

Benji lifted his eyes hopefully. "So...we're not getting detention?"

Dorian leaned back with another laugh. "Oh, no—you're *definitely* getting detention. You're also going to make sure I don't get charged for any damages done to that door. But I still thank you."

Aria bit her lip, thinking it over. Yes, the punishment sucked, but if the night had proven anything it was that they weren't wrong in thinking Dorian was the intended target.

Now if they could just figure out who the attacker was...

"So you really have no idea who would come after you?" she pressed coaxingly. "A disgruntled former student, or employer, or landlord, or even a wife—" She caught herself quickly, paling on the spot. "Not that it's any of my—I mean, our—business..."

Benji's right. I have to stop watching so many crime dramas.

Dorian's eyes twinkled as he slipped the glasses back onto his face.

"*No*, it is not." He let it hang for a moment, walking to the kitchen to put on the kettle for more tea. "But as it happens I got along brilliantly with my students, owned my own house, and received a glowing reference from my former employer for this job." His eyes flashed up with a wry smile. "And I've never been married."

She blushed to the roots of her hair, vowing to never speak again.

"Was there a particular reason you thought I'd have so many people out to kill me?" he asked curiously, pulling down a handful of mugs and then looked at Benji. "You know, instead of your father?"

Benji smiled self-consciously before lifting his shoulder in a shrug. "Only two people taught history, and they say Dorf had no social life outside the school. If he'd made any enemies it would have been sometime in his teens, and I highly doubt they'd be hanging on to a grudge this long. And when it comes to my dad..." He trailed off a moment, shrugging once again. "To be honest, I'd be more worried for the assassin."

The three shifters looked at him strangely, but the rest of them understood. There had been several close calls over the years, but the Kerrigan gang lived up to their legend. It would be a fool who'd choose to cross them now. Those few times it had happened ended very badly—for the attacker. Angel had once retaliated with such vengeance Molly sent flowers to the guy's grave.

"But you'd be worried about me?" Dorian asked with a trace of humor.

Benji flushed, staring down at the floor. "I-I didn't mean..."

"Our parents have years of training," Lily ventured tentatively. "And they always act like someone's after them—whether they are or not. You were the librarian. We wanted to help."

The second the words left her mouth, she looked like she immediately wished she hadn't spoken. But Dorian softened with an instant smile, offering a mug of tea.

"Like I said, it's the thought that counts. That was very...considerate of you."

"But we're still getting detention," Alexander muttered.

Dorian lifted his head with a sharp smile. "Yes, Mr. Hastings. For sneaking out after curfew and breaking down a teacher's door, I am obliged to give you at least one detention. Unless there's anything else you'd like to add to the list?"

The shifter paled, and dropped his gaze quickly. "No, sir."

A silence descended on the room. One broken only by occasional sips as the friends attempted to drain their scalding tea. In hindsight, it would look quite comical—kicking down the door only to be rewarded five minutes later with a cup of Earl Grey. In the moment, all Aria could think was how the Council had already failed. The man who'd attacked Dorf had been on campus not once, but twice. A third time seemed almost inevitable. But would it be the last?

"Is that a halberd?" James said suddenly, pushing to his feet.

Aria watched as he crossed to the bookshelf, tugging lightly on a wooden handle peeking from the side. Sure enough the spear fell into his hand a moment later, glistening and new.

"Yes, it is." Dorian pushed to his feet as well, setting his cup on the saucer. "I'm surprised you recognized it. Most people wouldn't. It's a bit old-fashioned now."

James gave it a cursory twirl, catching it lightly in his hand. "No—these are awesome," he answered excitedly. "My dad used to let Arie and me play with them in the backyard. Then my mom came home early one day..."

The others chuckled as Dorian approached him with an appreciative smile. "You handle it well. Looks like the lessons sank in."

James handed it back with a blush. "Sorry, I didn't mean to push in."

"Not at all—these things are meant to be used." Dorian flipped it effortlessly in the air before lunging with a playful thrust. The blade grazed the front of James' shirt. "My schedule's so busy now with the school, I barely get the time to practice."

James let out a breathless laugh, stepping carefully out of reach. Jason walked up behind them, staring at a pair of mounted scimitars on the wall.

"Sixteenth century," he murmured. "Perfect condition." He cocked his head as he spotted a chip in the handle. "Well, almost. Where did you get these?"

"From my sister," Dorian answered, taking them off their hooks and placing them in Jason's reverent hands. "She was a bit of collector. When she died, her things all went to me."

Jason sliced one quickly through the air, listening with a grin to the deadly hiss. "These are fantastic. Your sister had really good taste."

Dorian flashed a quick smile. "She'd have been pleased to hear it." His eyes flickered without thinking to a chest in the corner, one that assumedly held more of the collection. "At first, I didn't see the point of lugging it with me wherever I go. Now, with someone breaking in to campus, I'm glad I did."

The friends looked up slowly as the implication slowly sank in.

"But you wouldn't..." Aria trailed off nervously. "You wouldn't fight them yourself, would you?" She happened to know the attacker was gifted with some kind of supernatural speed. All the weapons in the world wouldn't help with that. "I mean...we don't even know your ink."

The teacher lifted his head in surprise, and her cheeks flamed with a blush. It was the second time she'd crossed a line without thinking. If possible, this was even more personal than the first.

You never knew how someone was going to react to that question. Most people grew up knowing exactly what was coming and wore their tatù with pride. But others found it difficult to talk about—especially if it was a set of passive ink. Most times, it was best to let it come up naturally.

"Dude," Benji chided, elbowing her sharply in the ribs. "Shut up."

The rest of them looked similarly mortified on her behalf, but Dorian was studying her face with a curious smile. A second later, he started rolling up his sleeve.

"I'm a telepath."

Aria nodded apologetically, eyes flickering to the ink on his arm. It looked similar to Catalina's, her roommate. Just with a bit more shading and complication around the edges.

"That's cool," she said quickly. "I got that from my mom as well."

Dorian's eyes twinkled as he rolled down his sleeve. "I'm sure you did. I'm sure you've gotten all sorts of things." He cocked his head curiously to the side. "No limitations, right? You can absorb, retain, and use anything simultaneously?"

She nodded again as Benji lowered his voice to a comical whisper.

"We try not to talk about it. Her ego's impossible enough as it is."

The teacher smiled, taking the halberd resting against the desk now and slipping it back behind the shelf. "I would imagine it hasn't been easy for any of you. Once they lifted the ban on hybrids, your generation was always in for a bit of a rocky road. Fascinating, though. Endless possibility."

Given how much controversy there still was in the supernatural community, it was nice to hear such a refreshing take. Yes—endless possibility. Why couldn't most people just leave it there?

"Even you," he added suddenly, giving James a nudge. "You must be terribly excited."

James looked up in surprise, then froze uncomfortably. Since the day he was born the question had weighed heavy on his mind. But he almost never talked about it.

"I don't know," he mumbled. "I mean, chances are I won't get anything." His eyes flashed resentfully to his older sister. "Arie already got the gene."

The others glanced self-consciously at their feet, but Dorian remained completely immune.

"Oh, I don't know about that. The more people with ink are intermarrying, the more that's starting to change. Take these two, for example. Brother and sister, but they both have the gene. Right, Sophie?"

Aria's head snapped up, following his gaze in surprise. Yes, things were technically starting to change, but not that fast. It was almost unheard of that two children in the same family would possess the gene. She'd just assumed that they were only half-siblings, like her mother and Kraigan.

"Is that true?" Benji asked incredulously, having assumed the same thing. "You guys are fully related, but you both shift?"

Alexander and Sofia exchanged a quick glance.

"Yeah, we do. But we're twins," he added suddenly. "So maybe that's different."

The hopeful smile slipped off James' face as his eyes dropped to the floor. Aria was about to say something, when the spotlight suddenly shifted back onto her.

"So we've covered marital status and ink." Dorian lifted his eyebrows, turning towards her with an amused smile. "Anything else you want to ask me?"

Every instinct told her to stop. She *absolutely* should have stopped. But she kept going.

"How were you planning on stopping the murderer?"

This time it was too much.

"*What is that matter with you?*" Lily hissed.

"*Shut up,*" Jason added under his breath.

Benji shocked her in the ribs for good measure.

"Sorry about my sister," James deflected apologetically. "Ever since the accident at the zoo, she hasn't been herself."

Dorian stared at them incredulously, then let out a sudden laugh—easing the tension in the room. When he was finished he was still smiling, eyes twinkling as he looked them up and down.

"You want to know what I was planning?"

All eight of them froze, then nodded in perfect unison.

"Let me show you..."

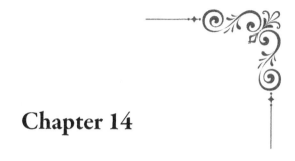

Chapter 14

Some kids grew up at daycare, looking at picture books and playing dress-up. Aria and her friends grew up in the Oratory—watching trained agents try to beat each other to death.

There wasn't an inch of the giant training circle they didn't know. There wasn't an inch they hadn't sparred on themselves. Since they were four years old and gave each other boosts up to reach the weapons, they'd made the space their own. Sparring on the upper levels, filling the secret lower levels with finger-paintings and empty juice boxes from their time spent below ground.

The point being, when Dorian led them to the Oratory that night they shouldn't have been surprised. They shouldn't have frozen in the doorway, or watched with wide incredulous eyes as he turned on the lights. It made sense for the three shifters to be acting that way, but not the friends.

And yet, from the moment the door swung open, they found themselves completely stuck.

"This way," Dorian cocked his head towards the training mats, still carrying the giant chest of weapons under his arm. "Why so nervous? I would have thought you'd been here tons of times."

"We have," Aria said carefully, stepping over the threshold. "Just...not like this."

Truth be told, she wasn't exactly sure what 'this' was. As a member of the Guilder faculty, Dorian was perfectly entitled to use the facility any time he wanted. The key had been presented his first day, and the doors were open day and night. That being said, he wasn't a member of the Privy Council. Furthermore, no other members of the Privy Council happened to be training there that night. The place was completely deserted, save for the eight teenagers lingering by the door.

Dorian glanced over his shoulder, then dropped the chest onto the mats with a chuckle. "You feel another detention coming on?"

A smile flickered through the friends as they relaxed ever so slightly, filing inside and shutting the door firmly behind them. Yes, it felt strange to have come uninvited. Especially without an agent. Especially given that all eight of them were breaking curfew after dark.

"You're allowed to bring students?" Sofia asked lightly.

Dorian glanced up again and seemed to sense that reassurances were required. "I might be new, but I'm fairly certain I can invite whomever I choose. I'm also certain that you charming truants are allowed to break curfew as long as it's within my supervision."

When they continued to hesitate he leaned back on his heels, staring at them in surprise.

"I'm sorry if I misread your interest. If you'd rather go back to the dorms—"

"No," Benji said quickly, crossing the mats to join him. "This is cool." He knelt down tentatively, fingers grazing the edge of the chest. "May I?"

Dorian smiled, and gestured him forward. "Be my guest."

The second the mystery box was open, the others flooded towards it. In an ironic way, the supernatural community bred a bit of a warrior culture. While the PC's doctrine was to promote peace and harmony, they did so through a blinding show of force. The children had been born into that mindset just like the rest of them. Weapons weren't just dangerous...they were toys.

Probably why he keeps them in a chest.

"Dude, this is awesome..." Benji muttered, lifting the pieces out carefully to see what was underneath. "Is that a dual-bladed chakram?"

Aria was kneeling just behind him, aching to touch it herself.

"Sure is." Dorian tilted his head, watching them with a faint smile. "You ever try one?"

Benji shook his head, running a finger along the edge. A tiny cut opened along the inside, smearing the skin with blood. "Not like that. Ours were smaller, with the uh..."

"The crosspiece?"

"Yeah." He held it up with a frown, gauging the balance. "How do you even grip?"

"Like this." Dorian skillfully slipped his hand inside the middle, giving it a twirl with his opposite hand. "I trained with the smaller version myself, but this can do more damage."

With that, he let it fly straight towards the dummies on the far wall. There was a whizzing *slice* as a severed head fell to the ground.

The friends stared in shock, then turned back to their teacher with a sort of awe.

"You're a *telepath*?" Benji asked incredulously.

Dorian laughed, clapping him on the shoulder. "Even librarians know how to have a bit of fun."

FOR THE NEXT FEW HOURS, the friends delighted in the wonders of an abandoned Oratory and a lethal chest of toys. Dorian participated occasionally, each time stunning them with a flash of truly unfathomable skill. But for the most part, he leaned back against the wall and let them have the run of the place—playing out secret war games and fulfilling deadly fantasies to their hearts' content.

Ironically enough, it was the only thing that could have brought them together.

The fight was forgotten. The feelings that caused it disappeared. For a few stolen hours in the middle of the night the eight teenagers forgot that they'd almost killed each other, and tried killing each other all over again. Only with slightly less blood and screaming. *Slightly.*

"Oh come on!" Jason sprinted across the mats then dove into a rolling somersault, just as a serrated javelin soared over his head. "What the he—heck is that!"

Aria flashed a breathless grin, giving the second spear a threatening twirl. "You said we could choose our own weapons."

He pushed to his feet, jogging over with a laugh. "Yeah, but I said it when you were holding a pair of throwing stars. How was I supposed to know you'd set them down and go for the heavy artillery?"

She bit her lip, levitating the spear just out of reach. "*That* is a question I imagine you'll be asking for a long time..."

On the other side of the room, things were heating up between Benji and Sofia—both of whom had found themselves reaching for the same set of daggers. He'd conceded them with a gentlemanly nod, then leapt back with a shout as she gave one an expert twirl and stabbed it through the sleeve of his jacket. There'd been a charged moment where neither of them said a thing. Then a mangled zipper fell to the floor and both of them began to smile.

It was the closest either would ever get to an apology.

As it stood, they'd separated a bit away from the others and were using the crossbow to shoot targets on the other side of the room. Rather, Benji was shooting targets. Sofia was trying.

"You're supposed to aim for the center," he said innocently. "Not the side—"

"If you don't be quiet, I'll aim for the center of you."

She let loose another arrow, only to have it bury itself in the outer rim. He pursed his lips and dropped his eyes to the ground, while she turned with a slow glare.

"Not a word, Fodder."

"I wouldn't dream of it."

Another arrow flew. This one vanished into the wall.

"*Perfect.*"

"Shut up."

"No, I think you hit a fly."

She snorted in laughter, then shot him a rueful grin. "Show me?"

With a little smile, he came up behind her—guiding her hands. "All you need is to relax..."

Together, they loaded the bow and tried again as Aria and Jason watched with matching grins from the far wall. They didn't even notice Alexander until he was standing by their side.

"Well, this is precious."

They threw him a glance, but found it surprisingly easy to shrug off as they turned their attention back to the targets. Around the fourth or fifth time they'd squared off against the shifter, lunging with daggers or hurling deadly spears, some of the controversy had begun to wear off.

"Shut up—there's nothing weird," Aria said dismissively. "He's just helping her."

"My sister hasn't missed the bullseye since she was nine years old." *...oh.*

Aria's eyes strayed once more to where Benji and Sofia were laughing quietly, his long arms running alongside hers as they leveled the arrow at the target. Before they could let go, she turned back to Alexander with a curious frown.

"And why is that?"

It was easy to ask the question privately, given that Dorian was currently showing Lily and James a collapsible scythe, and after having spent the last few hours together there was really no avoiding it. It wasn't just that his sister was apparently a flawless shot, he and Eric were confident handling most of the weapons that had come out of the chest as well. And it wasn't that they'd received training, per se. There was a rawness to the way they moved that spoke to most everything being self-taught. But there was talent there nonetheless. And experience.

"What do you mean?" he stalled, wishing he hadn't walked over.

"The three of you..." Aria paused, wondering how to say it.

She hadn't told anyone the secret Sofia had shared the night of the attack. Strong as the urge was to spill every detail to her friends, she somehow felt the story wasn't hers to tell. But knowing what she did about the shifters' rather tragic origins, she couldn't see how weapons training fit.

Much to her surprise, Jason swooped in for the save.

"Our parents are freaks," he said with the hint of a grin. "Since we could walk they were showing us things like this. You three are good. How did that happen?"

Alexander's face lightened with a hint of surprise, but he betrayed no other emotion. Instead he gave the sword in his hand a quick twirl, eyes focused entirely on the movement.

"Stuff like this was always lying around when we were growing up. You spend enough unsupervised time with it, you pick up a few tricks. Of course, when we turned sixteen and got our ink there was hardly a need—"

He cut himself off quickly, shaken by what he'd almost said. There was a charged moment where no one spoke, then Jason's lips twitched with the world's most unlikely smile.

"I can vouch for that."

...seriously?

Aria's mouth fell open in astonishment, but he was already walking away—cocking his head as a silent invitation for her to follow. She hurried quickly after him, still blown away that he'd speak of such a thing so casually. But before they'd gone more than five steps, Alexander called after them.

"I'm sorry."

There was a hitch in Jason's step before he slowly turned around. The shifter was already standing behind him, looking as uncertain as Aria had ever seen. His lips parted suddenly, then froze, as if it was a physical torment to say the words. But he took a breath and forced on through.

"The other night in the woods...I'm sorry for attacking you. For letting things go so far."

Across the room, target practice came to a sudden halt as Benji and Sofia looked over at the same time. Both were gifted with advanced senses. Both couldn't believe what they'd just heard.

"You didn't deserve it," Alexander continued quietly, staring at the floor somewhere past Jason. "I didn't even want to...but I didn't know what you were planning with that ice."

In a kind of daze, Aria turned back to Jason—remembering the moment with perfect clarity.

The way a sudden chill had fallen over the clearing. The way his eyes turned silver and the air around him started to glow. She'd never seen anything more terrifying, or more beautiful. Her eyes flickered up to his fateful memento, a lock of shockingly silver hair.

"I wasn't planning to *tear you open* with it," Jason replied softly.

Alexander pulled in a tight breath, then bowed his head. "I know. I'm sorry."

A heavy silence fell between them. One that should have been impossible to break. But after a few drawn-out seconds, Jason nodded abruptly and gestured back to the chest.

"You guys up for round two?"

Just like that, the bloody night was behind them.

Just like that, another bloody night was about to begin.

After the chakrams came the nunchucks. Then came the crossbow. Then came a terrifying assortment of maces and pikes. When they were finished with those it was on to the throwing stars; the katanas and long swords were both on deck.

Dorian flitted from group to group, taking a step back when those groups occasionally merged together in order to observe. Although it was now in the early hours of the morning, he didn't appear impatient or tired. Quite the contrary, he watched their war games with a twinkling smile—vanishing only to procure a cup of coffee before returning to the mats.

"What's this?" James asked curiously, taking the final weapon from the chest. The sun was just beginning to peek above the horizon and the battles were finally winding down.

Dorian set down his empty mug and stepped forward, taking the strange-looking instrument from his hand. "It's called an urumi. They were used quite a bit back in India." He motioned for the children to step back, then lashed it into the air. "As quick as it is deadly."

Aria flinched back with an instinctual shiver. Never had she seen such a thing. The grip resembled that of a sword, but it was as if the blade had been cut into ribbons. Each one sliced through the air like a whip before flying back into Dorian's practiced hand.

The children stared with a quiet sort of deference. Talented as they might be themselves, the mild-mannered librarian was on a completely different level. The kind that made you do a double-take from across the room. The kind that demanded both caution and respect.

"Mr. Locke," Aria began tentatively, slipping back into formalities, "we're really sorry about the cottage door. We were just trying to...well, anyway, it's clear you don't need our help."

He lifted his eyes with a smile, putting the frightening weapon back in the chest. "Like I said, it's the thought that counts...*Miss Wardell.*"

She dropped her eyes with a grin.

"At any rate, everyone needs help from time to time. Like this," he said, gesturing to the various weapons strewn across the floor. "I never would have gotten these out if it weren't for all of you."

The children followed his gaze, abruptly sad they'd have to pack it all away.

"But I have a question," Dorian continued suddenly, eyes resting on each one. "If you were really convinced I was the killer's target...why didn't you report it to the Council?"

It was the million-dollar question. One with a simple and selfish answer.

"We probably should have," Aria mumbled, eyes on the floor. "But whenever we..." She trailed into silence, remembering all those hushed conversations. All those time she and the others had been sent outside to play. "We wanted to do this ourselves."

A sudden quiet fell over the Oratory as each of the friends acknowledged the unspoken truth. There was only so long they could wait on the sidelines. There was only so long they could linger invisibly in their parents' glorious shadow. More than anything in the world they wanted their own page in the history books, to leave something behind written in their own name.

A legacy of their very own.

Dorian watched them quietly, eyes resting on each one. "And you think you're up for the challenge?"

Before that evening, Aria might have actually said yes. The one thing they'd proudly inherited from their parents was an absurd amount of confidence that they tended to wear on their sleeves. But after seeing glimpses of Dorian? The sheer difference in skill?

"No," she said softly, "probably not."

A little smile crept up the man's face, growing brighter every second.

"In that case, we'll have to train a little harder."

The others lifted their heads at the same time, throwing each other looks of confusion. Sure they hadn't heard correctly, sure they'd misunderstood. Benji stepped forward, shaking his head.

"...what do you mean?"

Dorian stared at them another moment before flipping the chest shut. "Same time tomorrow?"

Chapter 15

The next few days were like something out of a dream—a dream they had been waiting for all their lives.

The second classes were dismissed Aria and her friends would race back to the dorms, rushing through as much of their homework as was technically required. Then would tea back outside again and trek down the grassy path to Dorian's cottage.

From there, the routine was simple. He would greet them, offer them tea. They would decline. Then the whole troop of them would head outside to cheerfully beat each other to death.

At first, they'd thought it would be better to keep meeting after dark in the Oratory. While there was nothing technically illegal about what they were doing, it still felt strange to be meeting with a teacher, not a trainer, and using the PC training grounds to do it. The cognitive dissonance was so strong that, by the same collective instinct, they'd all conveniently neglected to mention said training to either Carter, Tristan, or their parents. But the second time that one of them fell asleep in their morning classes, having been awake all night dodging spears, they'd decided on a change.

The cottage Dorian had been granted by the school was conveniently distanced from the others. It was also on the very edge of the tree-line, meaning that instead of training right out in the open they could simply wander several paces up the hill to a little clearing. The fresh air was better than the smell of practice mats, and the distance from the school helped a great deal with the noise. Of course, if the students of Guilder listened hard enough they could still hear the shouts.

"Again!"

The friends stood in a line, watching as Jason and Lily slowly circled each other, drenched in sweat, the cuffs off their sweatshirts stained in blood. Each one was wielding a deadly khopesh—an Egyptian blade with a notch in the middle used for either decapitating or disarming one's opponent.

There had been several close calls on both counts.

"What's the matter, Decker?" Jason taunted, spinning the handle so the late afternoon sun glinted off the blade. "Scared?"

She tightened her grip with a chilling smile. "Just waiting on you, princess. Think it through, take your time."

There was a fierce cry and they charged forward again, swinging at each other with the long, curving strokes that Dorian had shown them just an hour earlier. The sound of metal crashing against metal rang through the air as they twisted and spun, wielding the savage blades without mercy. Both trying fiercely to get the upper hand.

It was bloodier and more dangerous than anything they'd done before—a definite escalation from the previous days' battles. At any moment Aria expected Dorian to step in and intercede, but the man was watching with just as much intensity as they were themselves. Eyes dilated with absolute focus as they followed the children's every move.

"On your left," he warned Lily, nodding with approval as she flipped out of the way. "It's not going to lift itself, Jason. You've got to swing it higher."

Jason nodded quickly, panting with exertion as he hurried to do as his teacher asked. There was another deafening *clang* as the friends crashed together, fighting with all their might.

Perhaps the reason for the new level of tension was that, before the match, Dorian had stepped forward and removed the thin strip of rubber covering both blades. It was the equivalent of using bullets instead of blanks. Suddenly, if one of the people sparring forgot to duck or failed to move quickly enough, they wouldn't get a welt. They'd get a cut. A deep one. Possibly fatal.

These weapons weren't designed to hurt, they were designed to kill. And the children were certainly swinging them with enough force to do so. Perhaps that was also the reason that every few seconds, either Benji, or James, or Aria would cast a nervous look towards the school.

What would they say if they saw us? How could we explain something like this?

"Stop pulling your punches!" Lily demanded, dropping down to the grass and kicking Jason's legs out from under him with a sweep of her own. "Let's go—for real!"

At first the kids had been thrilled. Then they'd been terrified. In the end they'd settled somewhere in between the two. At times surges of adrenaline would take them, and they'd find themselves throwing caution to the wind and battling full force. Other times, one of them would land a strike on the other and pale at the blood. The intensity would immediately slacken. The looks towards the school would triple as they each silently wondered if what they were doing was okay.

Jason was having a particularly hard time battling Lily. For the last thirteen years of his life, he'd come to regard the girl as a little sister—and he didn't *do* 'siblings' like Aria and James. The guy was fiercely protective. *Fiercely.* And here he was hacking away at her with a blade.

"Look at how I'm standing," he panted quietly, "with all the balance on my front foot. Now's the time that you should lunge—"

"Are you serious?" she demanded, abandoning the weapons altogether and lobbing a punch at his face. "Stop *helping* me, genius. Fight back!"

Benji leaned towards Aria with a hidden smile "This is definitely the kind of thing we should start placing money on..."

She snorted with laughter, keeping her eyes on the fight.

There had been several memorable moments over the last few days—but none where she'd feel comfortable placing bets. You simply never knew what was going to happen until you set foot inside the ring. You never knew what your opponent was going to bring to the table.

"Move your feet, Lily," Dorian commanded, guiding them through the motions with the skill of a seasoned general. "Jason—extend your arm. Yes, that's much better."

Their progress had surged and waned, but the one thing that had remained consistent was Dorian. Less than a month he'd been at the school, but already Aria didn't know how they'd ever lived without him. He could be stern as Commander Fodder one minute, then playful the next. At no point did she ever feel like they were in real danger under his watchful eyes, and yet there was a sense of risk about everything they were doing. The thrill of untapped potential they'd yet to unlock.

At last, when Jason and Lily had battled long enough, Aria switched into her uncle's metal-manipulation tatù and flicked her fingers. Wrenching the blades out of their hands and into the sky.

"Enough," she said bluntly. "My turn."

Dorian chuckled as the others looked over in surprise. Needless to say, adrenaline had won out over caution and each of the friends was dying to try it themselves.

"Apologies," James said with a sarcastic roll of his eyes. "My sister never learned to share."

Lily and Jason stalked over to her, demanding that she lower the swords back into reach. But Dorian had already snapped his fingers, gesturing Aria and Sofia to the ring.

Finally.

The blades dropped into the girls' hands as they began moving in a slow circle, watching each other carefully to see who would make the first move. In the beginning, Aria hadn't liked being paired with the shifters. Not that she particularly minded them anymore—Alexander was still an ass, and Eric most definitely had some troll blood—it's just that she didn't *know* them. Didn't know the way they thought, couldn't predict their movements.

In the beginning she'd hated it. Now she appreciated that about them.

It made things more of a challenge.

"Anytime, Aria." Sofia gave the blade a quick twirl, placing one foot carefully in front of the other. "Unless you'd like to forfeit now."

There was a chuckle from the sidelines and even Aria had to smile.

When they'd first met, she'd written the girl off as impossibly shy. But there was grit buried just underneath that demanded admiration, along with a wicked sense of humor.

"I'm just deciding where to hit you first." Aria lifted her blade between them like a paintbrush, tilting her head to the side as she considered. "The left arm...or the right?"

"Girls—"

"You don't need the left arm much as a tiger, do you?" she asked innocently. "I mean, you have three others to spare."

"*Girls*," Dorian said again, fighting back a smile. "Much as I enjoy the posturing, you are in fact here to *train*. That involves a little more movement than just your mouths."

Aria looked at him seriously. "Sarcasm and intimidation are a crucial part of my battle strategy."

His eyebrow cocked with sarcasm as he nodded in reply. "Is another part losing?"

What—

Before she could see what was happening, Sofia had flipped her to the ground. All the air rushed out of her, but before she could suck in a breath the tip of the blade pressed into her throat.

She blinked up in surprise, ignoring the wild cheering from her friends. "I wasn't ready."

Sofia offered a hand, looking decidedly smug. "First mistake."

Even Aria had to grin as she ignored the hand and pushed defiantly to her feet. It wasn't in her nature to accept such things gracefully, but she had to admit the girl was a worthy opponent. One who needed to be cut down to size. With a flick of her telekinetic fingers, she summoned her fallen blade off the grass. But the second it reached her hand, she switched into a very different set of ink.

You want to fight as a shifter? Nothing faster than a cheetah...

In a blur of speed, she whipped around—slicing the sword through the air behind her. Only a shifter's reflexes allowed Sofia to jump back in time, but even then she didn't escape completely unscathed. The second their blades touched hers flew backwards, vibrating with impossible speed.

"Okay...*I* wasn't ready for *that*," she said ruefully, making her way to retrieve it.

Aria shrugged with a cocky smile. "First mistake."

Jason gave her a secret wink as Sofia joined her back in the ring.

"Oh—that was a *mistake*, was it?" She ducked the first swing Aria levelled at her and countered with one of her own. "Am I supposed to regularly anticipate something like that? How many people in the world can switch between sets of ink?"

"At least two," Aria said conversationally, levitating over her head in a supernatural flip before switching back to the cheetah when she touched ground. "But rest assured, our children can start a blood-feud and continue the fighting for years to come."

Sofia let out a laugh, but Dorian held up his hand.

"No extra powers, Arie. If you weren't sparring with a shifter, I'd say no powers at all."

The girls continued battling as Lily peered up at him.

"Why not?" she asked curiously. "Is it just because of tatù inhibitors? That someday we might find ourselves in a situation where our ink doesn't work?"

"That's a small part of it," Dorian answered. "But the simple answer is that if you're going to fight, you need to know how to *fight*. You need to be able to do it in your sleep, with one hand tied behind your back, with or without your powers. You can't rely on magic to save you. This stuff has to sink deep into your bones. It's the only way you win."

She nodded thoughtfully as James stared out at the fight with a bright smile. As the only person not guaranteed to ever *have* ink, he was thrilled by the notion that it might not necessarily be required. Benji glanced between the boy and the battle with a faint smile.

"But some of us can't turn it off."

He might not technically have been a shifter, but as someone who'd received the traits of a specific predator he was in exactly the same boat.

"No, you can't," Dorian agreed, eyes still on the battle. "And that's why I'm allowing Aria to use a tatù for this as well. Although...I don't think she picked a tiger."

There was another blur of speed, then Sofia was lying on her back. The ground cratered beneath her shoulders before she pushed to her feet with a painful grimace.

"Okay," she panted, "did I mention I was sorry for disarming you in the first round?"

"You're right," Jason stated, chuckling under his breath, "that was definitely faster than a tiger."

Faster, but not stronger.

The shifter maybe have acknowledged a momentary defeat, but she came back with a vengeance. No sooner had Dorian clapped that they should begin than she went tearing forward, dodging the swing of Aria's blade before full-on tackling her to the ground.

Jason lifted his eyebrows slowly, watching them roll around in the grass, while Alexander stifled a grin. Only Benji was unamused, planting his hands on his hips with a scowl.

"Arie, if you're going to spar with my ink—at least don't lose. It's embarrassing."

She managed a single glare before Sofia shoved her face into the ground. When she arose, spitting out a mouthful of grass in the most dignified way she could muster, she decided that blood-feud was going to start a little sooner than scheduled.

This time, she didn't wait for the clap. Faster than sight she flew off the ground, grabbing her sword in the same motion. Sofia spun around to meet her head-on, but the shifter wasn't fast enough. No sooner had she turned than Aria was standing behind her—kicking out her knees and felling her to the grass. A blade appeared at her throat. The match was called.

"Well done!" Dorian applauded, motioning for the girls to rise to their feet.

They did so with varying degrees of difficulty, grinning proudly as the rest of the friends applauded and cheered. It was nearing the end of hour four, and both were completely exhausted. If it weren't for the fact that Aria still had bits of grass in her mouth, she would have blacked out on the spot. As it stood, she lifted her hands proudly. Shoving Sofia when she tried to do the same.

"Nice," the shifter laughed. "Really classy."

Aria spat out a blade of grass.

Sofia laughed again, taking a second to catch her breath. She gave the blade a playful twirl, then paused and took another second. And another second after that.

The smile slowly faded from Aria's face.

"...Sofia?"

Benji pushed past before she could even finish asking the question, forgetting they had an audience and placing a hand on the shifter's back.

"It's all right," he murmured, steadying her gently. "Just breathe."

The others stared in confusion as she swayed dizzily, bringing a trembling hand to her face.

"I'm fine," she mumbled, though she didn't look it. A second later, she dropped the blade to the grass. "Really, it's just—"

"Let go." Alexander streaked forward from the sidelines, silently fuming as he took his sister from Benji's arms. "I got it."

Without another word he stepped between them, discreetly blocking her from view as he made a quick assessment. In the short time they'd been standing there her pulse had slackened, her breathing had sky-rocketed, and every speck of color had vanished from her cheeks.

He murmured a few words, she shook her head. Then, almost too fast to notice, he took a tiny syringe from his inner jacket pocket and pressed it covertly into the crook of her arm.

Her breathing slowed. Her eyes began to focus.

"That's it," he murmured, holding her by the upper arms. "Deep breaths."

Dorian was standing just a few feet behind them, watching the exchange in a state of frozen astonishment. The entire thing had happened so quickly, he was still getting over the shock of it when Alexander glanced over his shoulder—gesturing to the school.

"I think I'll take her back to the dorms, if that's okay."

The teacher stared at them for an incredulous moment before nodding quickly. "Yes, of course. Anything you need." His eyes tightened with concern as Alexander lifted his sister effortlessly into the air. "Sofia, I'm so sorry if we pushed too hard—"

"Not at all," Alexander cut in smoothly. "This was great. Thank you," he added abruptly, "for inviting us. We'll be back tomorrow."

Dorian nodded again, watching with a troubled expression as they started heading across the grass. Eric automatically lumbered to their side, and to Aria's surprise so did Benji. He might have been banned from actually carrying Sofia, but that did nothing to stop him from hovering.

"He's right, you'll be fine," he murmured under his breath, stroking her dark hair with a reassuring smile. "We'll just get you to the dorms and—"

"Get back," Alexander snapped, jerking sharply, knocking his hand away. "You're not a part of this."

Benji froze like the man had shocked him, watching as they walked away. His bright eyes shone with concern, but there was very little he could do. A moment later he rejoined the group.

"Well that, uh...was certainly unexpected." Dorian floundered in confusion, trying to think of something to say. "I don't suppose any of you know what's the matter?"

His eyes flashed automatically to Benji, but the boy shook his head much too quickly to be believable—convincing Aria at once that he *did* know. The rest of them were honestly in the dark, and she was about to make up an excuse on the girl's behalf, when Jason jumped in suddenly.

"I think she's just under the weather." The eyes of the group fell on him, but he gave a casual shrug. "This morning she thought she was coming down with the flu."

Dorian nodded slowly, in no way fooled, while Aria stared at her new boyfriend in shock.

He knows! I'm not sure how...but he definitely knows!

She couldn't imagine how it had happened. Not unless Benji had found out and told Jason about it himself. But for some reason, she didn't think that was the case. In fact, she had a sneaking suspicion that Jason had known the shifters' story before all the rest of them...

"Well, maybe it's best that we call it a day," Dorian said with forced lightness. "They'll be serving dinner soon, and the last thing you want is for some PC agent to catch you out of bed."

"Why not?" James asked with a grin. "We could put on a little demonstration."

He either didn't care about Sofia or had bought the flu story completely. Either way he'd already moved on in his head, twirling a bow staff while staring wistfully at the Oratory.

"Maybe they'll be so impressed, they'll offer a job."

The others chuckled, packing weapons back into the chest. But Dorian had gone very still, staring at the remaining teenagers with a peculiar expression on his face.

"And that's something you all want?"

"Are you kidding?" Aria exclaimed. "Joining the PC...that's *everything*."

With no further prompting, the five friends launched into a spirited discussion of how life would change once they were finally invited inside those hallowed doors. Of course, the entire thing was rife with speculation and hypotheticals, but that did nothing to dampen their enthusiasm as the conversation soared to greater and greater heights. The missions they would have, the places they would go, the things they'd finally be allowed to do with their powers.

That, in particular, was a source of particular excitement.

"It's already starting," Aria said importantly, "even without training. In the woods that night, Jase—you were *glowing*. There's no telling what might have happened if you hadn't been..." She wisely chose to switch the subject. "And Benji, your eyes? I've never seen them light up like that."

"That was pretty damn impressive," Jason agreed appreciatively, throwing his friend a quick grin. "To be honest, you reminded me of your mom."

In their world, there was no bigger compliment. But Benji was too distracted to hear it. He nodded absentmindedly, still shooting worried looks at the dorms.

"Yeah, I know. I've been trying to recreate it, but so far no luck. Maybe I just need..." He caught himself just like Aria, flashing a faint grin. "...to be *really* motivated."

Lily rolled her eyes, while James masked his laughter in his sleeve. *Nothing says motivation like fighting off a bloodthirsty tiger.*

"And that's all without formal training," Aria insisted, circling back to the point. "Just imagine what it's going to be like once we've been assigned someone to help."

Dorian frowned ever so slightly, glancing at Jason. "Your dad didn't have formal training."

"He's had it since," Jason answered, dumping an armful of daggers into the chest, "and he *loved* it. Couldn't stop talking about all these things he'd missed. Different styles and techniques. The fundamentals—"

"—of a proper education," all the children finished in unison.

They'd heard the same speech from their own parents many times before.

Dorian watched them a second longer, quiet understanding flickering in his eyes.

"You *really* want all that, don't you?" he asked softly.

Lily flashed a bright smile. "Of course we do. Why wouldn't we?"

Dorian just shook his head and waved them off. "You kids get back inside, I'll finish up here."

"Are you sure?" James asked in surprise. "We can help clean up."

"Don't worry about it. Get some dinner. And some rest."

They dropped what they were holding and headed back to the dorms, still buzzing with adrenaline over the events of the day. Halfway there, Aria glanced over her shoulder.

"Same time tomorrow?"

Dorian stared a moment, then inclined his head. "Same time."

With that the friends traipsed happily across the grass as the sun slipped quietly behind the trees, having no idea what other adventures the night had in store...

————————⟨◊⟩————————

IT HAPPENED ALMOST immediately, the second they were out of sight. One moment, the friends were heading up to the cafeteria, congratulating themselves for being on time for once and wondering if their classmates would notice all the blood. The next, they were surrounded.

"Good evening."

Aria froze in her tracks as a pair of men materialized right in front of her. Dark clothes, regulation weapons, and the same smirking faces she'd had the honor of seeing before.

Oh, crap.

She was still in the cheetah tatù, but before she could even say a word four more agents appeared behind her, cutting her off from the rest of her friends. A panicked breath caught in her chest as all that confidence she'd been building during training vanished.

"What-what is this?"

Maize took a step closer, smiling down with a look of hungry anticipation in his eyes. "This, my dear, is called a murder investigation. I'm not surprised you don't recognize it, given that we haven't been allowed to actually investigate. Even though you were the only person present at the time of a violent crime, we've yet to even interrogate you...until now."

Her breathing hitched as a sudden chill ran down her spine.

While she might not have had anything to do with Professor Dorf's murder, she'd certainly done many things since then she was sure the stern hand of the Privy Council wouldn't allow. And it wasn't just her secrets she'd be spilling. It was the secrets of every single one of her friends. If it wasn't their covert training sessions after school, or the midnight fiasco that had started them, it was the knowledge that Alexander Hastings had almost ripped a fellow student in half.

The boy was of legal age and an outsider. He would not receive a trial. He would disappear.

"She's already answered the Council's questions," Jason said angrily, pushing his way through the agents to stand by her side. "The president himself cleared her."

Maize chuckled under his breath, as if the boy's defiance amused him. "The *president* cleared his *granddaughter*," he clarified. "He then told us to complete a thorough investigation. That's exactly what this is. We're covering all the bases. Tying up loose ends."

Lily shook her head darkly, eyes burning with rage. "And what do you hope to gain by doing this?" she asked quietly. "The leader of your own agency is against you. There is no endgame here. Even if you win—you lose."

Windall leaned down, bringing himself even with her eyes. "Sometimes it's not about winning or losing, little girl. It's about proving a simple point."

She clenched her teeth, staring back without a hint of fear. "And that point is?"

"That the Privy Council isn't a family business," Maize said briskly. "It's an international intelligence agency and it's time it starting acting like one. Grandfathers should not have the legal authority to clear their grandchildren. Mothers should not have the authority to clear their sons. If this were any other case it would have been an open and shut investigation, but because it involves the five of you..." His eyes sparked with anticipation. "Well, let's just say that ends tonight."

He took a step closer and Aria found herself genuinely terrified as to what was going to happen next. It wasn't like she could fight him; it wasn't like she could run. And after breaking into the library to read a mountain of classified case files, she had a keen understanding of exactly what happened to the suspects of an open investigation if the interrogation didn't go their way.

"You can't force me to say anything," she blurted, taking an instinctual step back. "Not without one of my parents present. I'll help you out and give them a call—"

The phone was snatched out of her hand before she had a chance to push the first button.

"There's no need for parental representation," Maize said with a smile, crushing the metal in his bare hands. "You're over eighteen. The only ones we'd have a problem interrogating would be Miss Decker and Mr. Wardell—and they happened to be the only ones not present that night."

Aria shrank back a step further, feeling Jason stiffen by her side. The agents had chosen their moment perfectly—they were caught between the cottages and the school. No hope of intervention, no chance of anyone stumbling upon them to witness the blessed event.

"So you won't be interrogating me?" James asked boldly, eyes flashing around the circle. He was just as tall as most of the men standing around him, but less bulky—with a youthful, almost boyish frame. "In that case—I'll just head back to my dorm." His voice sharpened angrily. "Or *maybe*...maybe I'll go visit my grandpa instead. See what he has to say about all this."

"Carter isn't here," Windall answered with a smile. "Neither is Tristan. Neither is Luke. If I'm not mistaken, your Uncle Gabriel has vacated the premises as well."

Aria glanced instinctively at the main gate, hoping for a last-minute rescue, only to see it tilted slightly off its hinges. The air shimmered where there was a break in the force-field, just a crack, but she was positive it had never looked like that before.

"Why is—"

"Fine," James backed away towards Joist, grabbing Lily by the wrist, "then we'll just go inside and get some dinner. That shouldn't be a problem, since you have no technical reason to keep us here—"

Two more agents sprang out of the darkness, catching them in the blink of an eye. Aria let out a furious cry, but it was too late. Before they could even struggle, they were lifted so the tips of their toes were barely touching the ground and their arms were pinned firmly behind their backs.

"—no reason except to prevent you from obstructing justice," Maize finished. "You think I don't know the two of you would go straight to the faculty lounge and sound the alarm, run to the Oratory and drag out whoever you could find?"

"Why do you care?" Lily hissed, straining against the hands that imprisoned her. "If you're just following Carter's orders, if your motives are so *pure*—why do you care who sees you do it?"

Maize paused, shot a quick look at his partner, then turned back with a smile. "For a second, I almost forgot who your father is. You sound just like him."

Her dark eyes flashed as her hands balled into fists. "You know my father? Then you should know he's going to *kick your a*—"

A gag was procured from nowhere and shoved roughly into her mouth. The second James tried to protest, he was gagged as well. But the aftershocks didn't stop there.

"What the hell are you doing?!" Benji shouted, eyes flashing a dangerous shade of blue. "Let them go! You said it yourself, they're not even a part of the investigation!"

"They are impeding it," Windall said calmly. "As you are dangerously close to doing yourself." He eyed the ripples of electricity moving up and down the boy's arms—his own fingers twitching restlessly against his thighs. "Just give me a reason, kid..."

But Benji was beyond reason. The sight of his two friends, bound and gagged, combined with Sofia's collapse and his own soon-to-be forced confession, had pushed him over the edge.

"This is *insane*!" he yelled. "They're not impeding anything and there's no reason to gag them!" He jabbed a finger at James. "He's *thirteen* years old! You really want to—"

But at that moment, Benji froze where he stood.

His lips parted with a silent gasp as he stared down at the little tears opening all over his skin. It was like he'd been caught in some kind of invisible net and it was dragging him backwards.

"I wouldn't fight it," Maize advised, looking almost bored—as if he'd seen the routine many times before. "It'll only hurt more."

There was another gasp and Benji took a deliberate step back—catching his breath as the twisted magic slowly released him. When it finally stopped, he was shivering.

"We didn't do anything to Professor Dorf," Aria said quickly, desperate to stop things before they could escalate even further. "And we didn't see anything either. We liked the guy. We have absolutely no reason in the world to lie about this."

Maize tore his eyes away from Benji.

"Then you have absolutely nothing to fear." He pulled a tiny glass vial from the pocket of his jacket, giving it a little shake. "We might not have anyone with your Aunt Natasha's skill in manipulating memory, but the Privy Council has ways of getting people to talk."

Aria paled white as a sheet, staring at the liquid splashing around inside.

"Just a few drops and you'll be spilling your darkest secrets," Maize continued softly, lowering his voice even further as he stared down at her with a smile. "And I see no reason to limit the conversation to the night of the murder. With your particular family connections, I'm sure you'll have lots of interesting things to say—"

"Like what?"

The agents whirled around as a lone figure walked out of the shadows.

A sudden silence descended upon the clearing, as if everyone standing there had forgotten how to breathe. The tension was overwhelming, but the woman didn't seem to mind. She continued approaching at a measured pace, billows of white hair catching the light of the rising moon.

"Aunt Angel," Aria gasped, "these men were just—"

Angel held up her hand. She'd taken full stock of the situation the moment she arrived, but her eyes would travel no further than her sixteen-year-old daughter. And the gag in her mouth.

"Miss Cross," Maize stammered, turning an ashen shade of grey. Like Aria's own mother, people often forgot Angel's married name in times of panic and reverted back to old monikers instead. "I wasn't...we weren't expecting to see you on campus tonight."

She didn't answer. She stared at him instead.

"Conner, release the girl at once," he continued, waving his hand as if these sorts of mix-ups happened all the time. "And the boy as well. There's no need for all of that."

Lily and James were let go the same instant. Their feet crashed to the ground, and their hands flew up to remove the gags from their mouths. The second she was free Lily stepped compulsively towards her mother, turning back to the man who'd given the order.

She walked right up in front of him, then placed the gag back in his hand. "This belongs to you."

Without another word, the rest of the children melted into the spaces left between the men and went to stand behind Angel. Just a single woman in a trench coat versus eight heavily-armed agents, but there wasn't a doubt in the world as to what exactly that woman could do.

Her face never changed as each one filed past. Her eyes never left Maize. But there was a comfort in the mere proximity, as if a life-raft had dropped down from the sky. Finally, when the only one remaining was Aria, she moved forward—taking the glass vial from his hand.

"And I thought they banned this."

The words were soft, no emotion whatsoever behind them, but the man looked like he'd taken a bullet to the chest. He floundered a moment, then made the extreme mistake of trying to rally.

"Not for use in official interrogations," he stammered, trying to remember the exact line. "In an active investigation, the prosecuting party may use whatever means necessary to—"

"That's what this is?" she asked quietly. "An official interrogation? With no record, no warrant, no witnesses? Just five teenagers in the middle of the lawn?"

The man fell silent, unable to speak.

"Kids...go inside."

They didn't need to be told twice. Without a backwards glance they left the entire terrifying scene behind them, racing into the darkness before they could hear the screams.

THE NEAREST BUILDING was the cafeteria, but none of them had the slightest appetite. For once, it had nothing to do with the smells wafting out of the building. Most of them simply couldn't stop shivering. Benji kept lifting a hand to his chest.

"Wait a second," Aria voiced, pulling them to a stop behind one of the towers. The temperature had dropped dramatically since they'd left Dorian's. The night had already begun to rain. "I know this is going to sound crazy, and I know you guys just want to get inside...but the gate is open."

Four faces went simultaneously blank.

"...the gate?" Jason finally managed, shaking his head. "Why do you care about the—"

"We know for a fact that someone's after Dorian," she interrupted. "Every agent who'd supposed to be on duty is getting beaten to death by Lily's mom. There is *no one* on patrol right now and...and the freaking gate is open!"

The others stared at her for a moment before Benji shook his head.

"No, I'm not doing this."

"Ben—"

"How many more close calls do you want?" he interrupted. "They almost made you drink that stuff, Arie. Right there on the lawn. You'd be spilling your guts right now about everything. About Alexander, about..."

"...about Sofia?" she finished caustically.

He shot her a glare, streams of water dripping down his face.

"I'd go with you anywhere. I'd see you through anything. But we *need* to get inside right now. Chances are Aunt Angel's the one who left the gate open."

"He's right," Jason said quietly, not quite meeting her gaze. "We need to leave, Arie."

Her eyes flew from one to the next, finding no help.

"I don't believe this," she cried. "You're going to make me go by myself?"

"I'll go with you."

She looked up in surprise as the others turned to James. Unlike the others, he hadn't brought a jacket to training and was shivering violently in the cold. But he made a concerted effort to stop when he saw them looking, drawing himself up to his full height.

"We'll check it out together," he said casually, "then head back to the dorms."

Their eyes met for a suspended moment as brother and sister shared a rare smile.

"Perfect," Aria said briskly, clapping her hands. "That settles it."

"No, it doesn't—" Benji began sharply.

"Get out of the rain. Take a hot shower." She flashed James another grin and gestured out to the dark. "We'll take care of this."

"Oh yeah?" Lily asked softly. "Just you and your baby brother? You're going to drag him off on the latest misadventure after he's just been caught and gagged by agents on the school lawn?"

The excitement faded in Aria's eyes before dying completely as she looked at James. There he was, wet and shivering, and willing to follow his older sister to the ends of the earth. But should she take him there? On a whim? On a night as dangerous as this?

"You're right," she said quietly, bowing her head, "we should get inside."

Benji threw up his hands.

"Finally, she sees reason."

"But we're going out to check it first thing in the morning," she retorted. "Even before our first classes, so you guys better not be planning on sleeping in—"

"Lily?"

The girl had frozen right in front of them, one hand still lifted towards the door. Unlike the rest of them, she no longer seemed to notice the temperature. She no longer seemed to notice much of anything. Her head was tilted to the side and a trickle of rain was running into her ear.

"*Lily*," Jason said again, circling around in front of her. Whatever he saw must have scared him, because his voice jumped an octave when he cried, "You guys—"

There was a sudden gasp as she stumbled forward, falling into his arms. Her fingers were twitching with strange rhythmic gestures, and a cloudy film was just clearing from her eyes.

"Honey." He lowered her gently, cupping a hand over her forehead to shield it from the rain. "Are you all right? What just happened?"

She blinked in disorientation, unable to believe what she'd seen. "...I just had a vision."

Aria fell to her knees beside them, mouth falling open in surprise.

"You did?" she gasped, looking down at the girl's twitching hand.

She's drawing, she realized. *She's trying to draw it out.*

"What was it?" Benji asked incredulously, kneeling on the other side. "Was it about me?"

Typical Benjamin.

Lily took another second to get her bearings, then shook her head.

"No...it wasn't about you at all. We've got to get to Dorian's."

All eyes flashed across the lawn before returning to the girl trembling on the ground.

"Why?" Aria said sharply. "Why do we need to go?"

Lily stared up at her, eyes wide with fright. "Because someone's about to die."

THE END

Coming Soon

The Kerrigan Kids Series

Book 1 - School of Potential
Book 2 - Myths & Magic
Book 3 - Kith & Kin
Book 4 - Playing With Power
Book 5 - Line of Ancestry
Book 6 - Descent of Hope

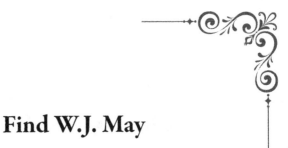

Find W.J. May

Website:
https://www.wjmaybooks.com
Facebook:
https://www.facebook.com/pages/Author-WJ-May-FAN-PAGE/141170442608149
Newsletter:
SIGN UP FOR W.J. May's Newsletter to find out about new releases, updates, cover reveals and even freebies!
http://eepurl.com/97aYf

The Chronicles of Kerrigan

B ook I - *Rae of Hope* is FREE!
   Book Trailer:
   http://www.youtube.com/watch?v=gILAwXxx8MU
   Book II - *Dark Nebula*
   Book Trailer:
   http://www.youtube.com/watch?v=Ca24STi_bFM
   Book III - *House of Cards*
   Book IV - *Royal Tea*
   Book V - *Under Fire*
   Book VI - *End in Sight*
   Book VII – *Hidden Darkness*
   Book VIII – *Twisted Together*
   Book IX – *Mark of Fate*
   Book X – *Strength & Power*
   Book XI – *Last One Standing*
   BOOK XII – *Rae of Light*

PREQUEL –

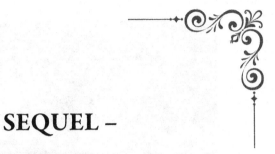

SEQUEL –

Matter of Time
Time Piece
Second Chance
Glitch in Time
Out Time
Precious Time

The Chronicles of Kerrigan: Gabriel

Living in the Past

Present for Today

Staring at the Future

More books by W.J. May

Hidden Secrets Saga:
Download Seventh Mark part 1 For FREE
Book Trailer:
http://www.youtube.com/watch?v=Y-_vVYC1gvo

LIKE MOST TEENAGERS, Rouge is trying to figure out who she is and what she wants to be. With little knowledge about her past, she has questions but has never tried to find the answers. Everything changes when she befriends a strangely intoxicating family. Siblings Grace and Michael, appear to have secrets which seem connected to Rouge. Her hunch is confirmed when a horrible incident occurs at an outdoor party. Rouge may be the only one who can find the answer.

An ancient journal, a Sioghra necklace and a special mark force life-altering decisions for a girl who grew up unprepared to fight for her life or others.

All secrets have a cost and Rouge's determination to find the truth can only lead to trouble...or something even more sinister.

RADIUM HALOS - THE SENSELESS SERIES
Book 1 is FREE:

Everyone needs to be a hero at one point in their life.

The small town of Elliot Lake will never be the same again.

Caught in a sudden thunderstorm, Zoe, a high school senior from Elliot Lake, and five of her friends take shelter in an abandoned uranium mine. Over the next few days, Zoe's hearing sharpens drastically, beyond what any normal human being can detect. She tells her friends, only to learn that four others have an increased sense as well. Only Kieran, the new boy from Scotland, isn't affected.

Fashioning themselves into superheroes, the group tries to stop the strange occurrences happening in their little town. Muggings, break-ins, disappearances, and murder begin to hit too close to home. It leads the team to think someone knows about their secret - someone who wants them all dead.

An incredulous group of heroes. A traitor in the midst. Some dreams are written in blood.

Courage Runs Red
The Blood Red Series
Book 1 is FREE

WHAT IF COURAGE WAS your only option?

When Kallie lands a college interview with the city's new hot-shot police officer, she has no idea everything in her life is about to change. The detective is young, handsome and seems to have an unnatural ability to stop the increasing local crime rate. Detective Liam's particular interest in Kallie sends her heart and head stumbling over each other.

When a raging blood feud between vampires' spills into her home, Kallie gets caught in the middle. Torn between love and family loyalty she must find the courage to fight what she fears the most and possibly risk everything, even if it means dying for those she loves.

Daughter of Darkness - Victoria
Only Death Could Stop Her Now
The Daughters of Darkness is a series of female heroines who may or may not know each other, but all have the same father, Vlad Montour. Victoria is a Hunter Vampire

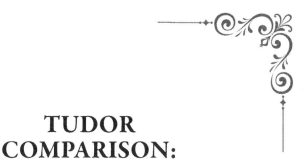

TUDOR COMPARISON:

Aumbry House—A recess to hold sacred vessels, often found in castle chapels.

Aumbry House was considered very special to hold the female students - their sacred vessels (especially Rae Kerrigan).

Joist House—A timber stretched from wall-to-wall to support floorboards.

Joist House was considered a building of support where the male students could support and help each other.

Oratory—A private chapel in a house.

Private education room in the school where the students were able to practice their gifting and improve their skills. Also used as a banquet - dance hall when needed.

Oriel—A projecting window in a wall; originally a form of porch, often of wood. The original bay windows of the Tudor period. Guilder College majority of windows were oriel.

Rae often felt her life was being watching through one of these windows. Hence the constant reference to them.

Refectory—A communal dining hall. Same termed used in Tudor times.

Scriptorium—A Medieval writing room in which scrolls were also housed.

Used for English classes and still store some of the older books from the Tudor reign (regarding tatùs).

Privy Council—Secret council and "arm of the government" similar to the CIA, etc.... In Tudor times, the Privy Council was King Henry's board of advisors and helped run the country.

Don't miss out!

Visit the website below and you can sign up to receive emails whenever W.J. May publishes a new book. There's no charge and no obligation.

https://books2read.com/r/B-A-SSF-NZECB

BOOKS 2 READ

Connecting independent readers to independent writers.

Did you love *Kith & Kin*? Then you should read *Discipline*[1] by W.J. May!

[2]

USA Today Bestselling author, W.J. May, brings you the highly anticipated continuation of the bestselling YA/NA series about love, betrayal, magic and fantasy.

Be prepared to fight, it's the only option.

Not every fairytale has a happily ever after...

For the first time in hundreds of years, the five kingdoms were at peace. United by the band of young heroes who'd won the Great War, the realm had entered a time of wealth and prosperity unlike anything it had known before. New families. New Beginnings. Old alliances were on the mend.

But such a thing can never last.

---

1. https://books2read.com/u/mBQaAk

2. https://books2read.com/u/mBQaAk

When Katerina and Dylan's teenage daughter finds herself at the center of a strange prediction, she and her friends are swept away on a wild adventure that may very well claim all of their lives. Old evils are lurking the shadows. A secret new darkness is waiting to take hold.

Can the new band of heroes stop it in time?

Or has their happily ever after finally come to an end?

Be careful who you trust.

Even the devil was once an angel.

OMEGA QUEEN SERIES

Discipline

Bravery

Courage

Conquer

Strength

Validation

ORIGINAL SERIES:

Queen's Alpha Series: Eternal

Everlasting

Unceasing

Evermore

Forever

Boundless

Prophecy

Protected

Foretelling

Revelation

Betrayal

Resolved

Read more at www.wjmaybooks.com.

Also by W.J. May

Bit-Lit Series
Lost Vampire
Cost of Blood
Price of Death

Blood Red Series
Courage Runs Red
The Night Watch
Marked by Courage
Forever Night
The Other Side of Fear
Blood Red Box Set Books #1-5

Daughters of Darkness: Victoria's Journey
Victoria
Huntress
Coveted (A Vampire & Paranormal Romance)
Twisted
Daughter of Darkness - Victoria - Box Set

Great Temptation Series
The Devil's Footsteps
Heaven's Command
Mortals Surrender

Hidden Secrets Saga
Seventh Mark - Part 1
Seventh Mark - Part 2
Marked By Destiny
Compelled
Fate's Intervention
Chosen Three
The Hidden Secrets Saga: The Complete Series

Kerrigan Chronicles
Stopping Time
A Passage of Time
Ticking Clock
Secrets in Time
Time in the City
Ultimate Future

Mending Magic Series
Lost Souls
Illusion of Power
Challenging the Dark

Castle of Power
Limits of Magic
Protectors of Light

Omega Queen Series
Discipline
Bravery
Courage

Paranormal Huntress Series
Never Look Back
Coven Master
Alpha's Permission
Blood Bonding
Oracle of Nightmares
Shadows in the Night
Paranormal Huntress BOX SET #1-3

Prophecy Series
Only the Beginning
White Winter
Secrets of Destiny

Royal Factions
The Price For Peace
The Cost for Surviving

The Chronicles of Kerrigan
Rae of Hope
Dark Nebula
House of Cards
Royal Tea
Under Fire
End in Sight
Hidden Darkness
Twisted Together
Mark of Fate
Strength & Power
Last One Standing
Rae of Light
The Chronicles of Kerrigan Box Set Books # 1 - 6

The Chronicles of Kerrigan: Gabriel
Living in the Past
Present For Today
Staring at the Future

The Chronicles of Kerrigan Prequel
Christmas Before the Magic
Question the Darkness
Into the Darkness
Fight the Darkness
Alone in the Darkness
Lost in Darkness
The Chronicles of Kerrigan Prequel Series Books #1-3

The Chronicles of Kerrigan Sequel
A Matter of Time
Time Piece
Second Chance
Glitch in Time
Our Time
Precious Time

The Hidden Secrets Saga
Seventh Mark (part 1 & 2)

The Kerrigan Kids
School of Potential
Myths & Magic
Kith & Kin
Playing With Power

The Queen's Alpha Series
Eternal
Everlasting
Unceasing
Evermore
Forever
Boundless
Prophecy
Protected

Foretelling
Revelation
Betrayal
Resolved

The Senseless Series
Radium Halos - Part 1
Radium Halos - Part 2
Nonsense
Perception
The Senseless - Box Set Books #1-4

Standalone
Shadow of Doubt (Part 1 & 2)
Five Shades of Fantasy
Shadow of Doubt - Part 1
Shadow of Doubt - Part 2
Four and a Half Shades of Fantasy
Dream Fighter
What Creeps in the Night
Forest of the Forbidden
Arcane Forest: A Fantasy Anthology
The First Fantasy Box Set

Watch for more at www.wjmaybooks.com.

About the Author

About W.J. May

Welcome to USA TODAY BESTSELLING author W.J. May's Page! SIGN UP for W.J. May's Newsletter to find out about new releases, updates, cover reveals and even freebies! http://eepurl.com/97aYf

Website: http://www.wjmaybooks.com

Facebook: http://www.facebook.com/pages/Author-WJ-May-FAN-PAGE/141170442608149?ref=hl *Please feel free to connect with me and share your comments. I love connecting with my readers.* W.J. May grew up in the fruit belt of Ontario. Crazy-happy childhood, she always has had a vivid imagination and loads of energy. After her father passed away in 2008, from a six-year battle with cancer (which she still believes he won the fight against), she began to write again. A passion she'd loved for years, but realized life was too short to keep putting it off. She is a writer of Young Adult, Fantasy Fiction and where ever else her little muses take her.

Read more at www.wjmaybooks.com.

Made in the USA
Monee, IL
05 April 2024

56402109R00125